# THE DECADENT
# TRAVELLER

MEDLAR LUCAN & DURIAN GRAY

# THE
# DECADENT
# TRAVELLER

*Edited by Alex Martin & Jerome Fletcher*

Dedalus

Published in the UK by Dedalus Ltd, Langford Lodge, St Judith's Lane, Sawtry, Cambs, PE17 5XE
email: DedalusLimited@compuserve.com

ISBN 1 873982 09 7

Dedalus is distributed in the United States from the 1st January 2001 by SCB Distributors,
15608 South New Century Drive, Gardena, California 90248
email: info@scbdistributors.com    web site: www.scbdistributors.com

Dedalus is distributed in Australia & New Zealand by Peribo Pty Ltd,
58 Beaumont Road, Mount Kuring-gai N.S.W. 2080
email: peribo@bigpond.com

Dedalus is distributed in Canada by Marginal Distribution,
Unit 102, 277 George Street North, Peterborough, Ontario, KJ9 3G9
email: marginal@ptbo.igs.net    web site: www.marginal.com

Dedalus is distributed in Italy by Apeiron Editoria & Distribuzione,
Localita Pantano, 00060 Sant'Oreste (Roma)
email: apeironeditori@hotmail.com

*First published by Dedalus in 2000*
Copyright © Medlar Lucan & Durian Gray
*Introduction copyright © Alex Martin & Jerome Fletcher 2000*

Typeset by RefineCatch Limited, Bungay, Suffolk

Printed in Finland by WS Bookwell

For Irma & Paul Renner

# THE AUTHORS

Since the publication of *The Decadent Cookbook* and *The Decadent Gardener*, Medlar Lucan and Durian Gray have been garlanded by critics and hounded by debt-collectors across the globe. Masters of disguise and deception, they have vanished from some of the world's greatest cities, including those described in the present volume. From time to time they appear in cabaret and at priapic festivals, offering a taste of their extreme cooking and eclectic lifestyle, based on their legendary Decadent Restaurant in Edinburgh. *The Decadent Traveller* fills in the 'missing years' between the *Cookbook* and the *Gardener*, and adds important new elements to their bizarre and alarming tale.

Lucan and Gray are currently living at El Periquito, a cabaret-brothel in Havana.

# Contents

# INTRODUCTION

Given the notoriety of the first two books produced by Medlar Lucan and Durian Gray, (*The Decadent Cookbook* and *The Decadent Gardener*) it was inevitable that the clamour for more of their peculiar brand of salaciousness would grow to the point where even they, reclusive and elusive as they are, would be compelled to produce the material for another volume. Public interest focused in particular on the period between the closure of the Decadent Restaurant, which brought about their expulsion from Edinburgh, and the moment when they arrived in Southern Ireland to start work on the gardens of Mrs Conchita Gordon's house at Mountcullen.

So, in response to the demands of a public desperate for the smallest scrap of information concerning the two debauchees, Lucan and Gray have once again provided us with a sackful of undigested material, a stinking pot-pourri of travel anecdotes, contentious opinions, lies, reminiscences, literary references, graphic – and often pornographic – diary entries, foreign phrases, left-luggage tickets and unpaid hotel bills. It has been our task to impose some sort of pattern on this material.

Whether we have succeeded in this, we must leave to others to judge. Now at least the events unfold according to the known laws of the physical universe: the travellers are in only one place at a time, they stay for a period before moving on, and time itself moves in a linear fashion (albeit with a few jumps and curves). But there the coherence ends: the narrative itself is shot through with uncertainty. We do not know for instance, whether Lucan and Gray actually travelled up the Nile, or visited the cave of the Ghost Children in Japan, or roamed the cemeteries of Buenos Aires in search of a dissolute uncle. These may be elaborate fictions. Yet such are the doubts that beset the reader of any travel narrative. It is a medium built for lying and exaggeration.

The story of Lucan and Gray's travels begins at the point where they were forced to leave the city of Edinburgh. Here they had spent many years carefully cultivating a scandalous reputation. However . . .

*'We were expelled from that city like two turds shat out through the sphincter of bourgeois morality. We were victims of persecution, no more no less, evicted from our home and forced to live, like all great visionaries, a life of exile.'*

This rather overwrought metaphor from the pen of Medlar Lucan gives a good idea of the bitterness he and Durian Gray felt about the unceremonious way in which they were hounded out of Edinburgh. It is an episode that is still shrouded in mystery, contradiction and myth-making, and it must be said that despite numerous attempts to set the record straight – in interviews, cabaret appearances and the like – Lucan and Gray have done little to elucidate the events of that fateful Sunday night. If anything they have added further layers of confusion to the existing chaos of disinformation.

Our own efforts to shed light on the matter – through the Edinburgh City Fathers, the police, Henderson's Debt Collection Agency and the official receivers, the firm of Goldberg, Tench and Van Rikkenbakker – have proved fruitless. Indeed, several of those approached clearly knew less than we did and were keen to find out more. Others knew more than was good for them and wished they could forget.

We decided finally that a touch of 'negative capability' – Keats's capacity for 'being in uncertainties, mysteries, doubts, without any irritable reaching after fact and reason' – was the most appropriate, indeed the only possible, response. A number of references in the present volume add detail and emotional colour to the record, but it essentially remains far from complete. Only four facts can be stated with any certainty.

1.  The police raided the Decadent Restaurant on Jan. 30th 1994.
2.  Lucan and Gray refused all bookings for the next three days.
3.  They disappeared without trace.
4.  A reluctant and ill-tempered alliance of creditors and city authorities was left to clear up the mess.

*Lucan and Gray before their journey. At this point The Decadent Restaurant was a still a going concern.*

According to the official police report, Lucan and Gray flew to London, then transferred to the first available cheap flight out of the UK, which happened to be for St Petersburg. It is at this point that the narrative of *The Decadent Traveller* proper begins.

Despite the tone of self-pity to be found in much of Lucan and Gray's writing at this period, their expulsion from the

Scottish capital was surely in some sense willed and positively sought by them. Although they were running a commercial enterprise with the usual commercial aims, they had another, hidden agenda, perhaps only half-conscious, which both contradicted and subverted their business goals: namely to outrage as many people in the city as possible. Their favourite and persistent targets were precisely the functionaries and legal officials (judges, senior policemen, government ministers, corporate executives) who, in their restaurant's heyday, were responsible for its success. Lucan and Gray were at first amused that such people found the restaurant congenial. Later they became worried and frustrated. They tried hard to drive them away, but only succeeded in attracting them in greater numbers. Even such innovations as the Circe room – a bare box with cement walls, concrete floor, a small trough in one corner and a ring in the middle to which clients were tethered naked, on all-fours, and fed massively overpriced pig swill – proved distressingly popular.

Their last desperate resort was to photograph these clients in moments of heedless abandon and then offer the pictures to various friends for their 'political edification'. Inevitably some photos found their way to the press. This finally did the trick, but it was widely seen as an act of betrayal and it spelt the end of the Decadent.

Lucan and Gray never ceased to complain that they were themselves victims of betrayal, but the reader would be entitled to treat such claims with scepticism. There always has been a streak of self-destructiveness in Lucan and Gray, and their efforts to provoke outrage are well documented.

As with their previous work, there are clearly two 'voices' audible in the writing. Indeed their personalities are here more individual than ever. They frequently have disagreements in the course of their travels, and part of the fascination of this assemblage of documents is the ebb and flow of tension, occasionally exploding into outright rage, between the two protagonists. There are moments when Medlar and Durian seem on the point of parting for ever, others where they are fused into a single

*Lucan and Gray in the Library at Mountcullen, posing as James Joyce and Augustus John. The picture was taken after the journeys described in this book.*

personality. There is something oddly reassuring about this tidal movement in their relationship, which seems to prove that no matter how determined a person may be (and they are extremely determined) to escape the common lot of humanity, the familiar strains and pressures assert themselves. To change the metaphor slightly, Lucan and Gray are divers without oxygen: it is not surprising that from time to time they come to the surface gasping for breath.

One of the difficulties of editing a 'manuscript' of this kind is in deciding what to omit, and on what grounds. We could not exclude material on grounds of obscenity, as this would have left the publishers with an unacceptably short book. The same applies to other criteria: irrelevance, inconsequentiality, inaccuracy, poor taste, crassness, and bad or overblown writing in general. All of these are endemic. We have therefore excluded only material that was illegible, defamatory or so fragmentary as to be nonsensical. Discarded chapter headings scrawled on cigarette packets, envelopes, pornographic post cards, etc. include 'Genghis Khan – The Father of Modern Tourism', 'The Sewers of Swindon', 'A Boy Scout's Guide to Bangkok', 'Around the World on Datura', and 'Sir Randolph Lederhosen – Gentleman, Traveller and Psychopath'. More complete, though no less bizarre, is the first chapter in this book: 'Purple Tourism – Our Philosophy of Travel'. Like everything else that Lucan and Gray turn their hand to, this chapter has a certain insane glamour. Deranged yet oddly stylish, it places one in a lotus-eating world of eccentric wealth and disinhibition – precisely the world of Mrs Conchita Gordon, whose offer of hospitality and employment as garden designers brought this strange and restless period of exile to a close.

JF
AM
South Mimms
May 2000

# PURPLE TOURISM
## An Essay on the Philosophy
## of Decadent Travel

The day Medlar and I were driven out of our beloved Edinburgh was one of the bleakest of our lives. Despair hung upon us like bitter black smoke and the darkness closed in over our heads. And yet, *de profundis*, we still managed to cling on to a scrap of consolation: the thought that our expulsion was at least in accord with our ideals of Decadence. At the restaurant we had often argued that to follow the path of true Decadence means to condemn oneself to a lifetime of rootlessness. The Decadent finds himself ejected from the society of Man and forced to wander aimlessly from one place to another in search of a home he knows he will never find. Our true vocation, we averred, was exile, a notion which has always appealed enormously to the Decadent imagination, and we too were drawn towards it as to a lodestone, compelled by the electro-magnetism of our souls.

Now we had been given the chance to live out our conviction. In this we saw ourselves following in the footsteps of a number of heroic literary, historical and mythical figures, among whom has to be counted Ahasuerus, the Wandering Jew.

Ahasuerus was a shoemaker by profession, outside whose shop the exhausted Christ paused to rest while dragging his cross along the Via Dolorosa. The cobbler's reaction was to give the Son of God a good kicking and tell him to clear off. (Not unreasonably, in our opinion. The sight of a blood-stained criminal collapsed under the weight of his own crucifix, thereby blocking the entrance to an establishment, can have a highly detrimental effect on one's livelihood. It was something we constantly had to guard against at the Decadent restaurant, where crucified individuals staggered past our door several times a week.) In reply, however, Christ cursed Ahasuerus, saying: '*I go quickly, but you will wait until I return.*' Yet more evidence of a God as mean-spirited and vindictive as an Edinburgh city councillor! Although we have no pretensions to eternal life of course we cannot help but have enormous sympathy for the man who was condemned in that moment to wander the face of the earth until Judgement Day. In this respect Ahasuerus came to resemble the figure who stands out as the very personification of the Exiled and the Rejected – Satan.

It would not be overstating the case to say that we revere Satan, just as he has been revered by Decadents of every age. This is not simply because he was the first and the most glorious of rebels, who paid for his rebellion by being exiled from the kingdom of God, but because in being exiled he was given no choice but to follow the path of evil. According to our theology (one which is imbued with a profound rationality) God *made* Satan evil by exiling him. Thus it is God who is responsible for unleashing evil upon the world. Charles Baudelaire, greatest of the French poets of the 19th century and a man who has long held an esteemed position in our Pantheon of Decadence, understood this perfectly. In *Les Litanies de Satan,* he addresses Satan thus:

> *O Prince de l'exil, à qui l'on a fait tort,*
> *Et qui, vaincu, toujours te redresses plus fort*
> *O Satan, prends pitié de ma longue misère!*
> . . .
> *Père adoptif de ceux qu'en sa noire colére*
> *Du paradis terrestre a chassés Dieu le Père*
> *O Satan, prends pitié de ma longue misère!*

> O Prince of Exile, who has been so wronged
> And who, vanquished, returns all the stronger.
> O Satan, have pity on my unending misery.
> . . .
> Adopted father of those whom God the Father
> in his black anger has hounded out of the earthly paradise,
> O Satan, have pity on my unending misery.

The divine Charles was something of an inspiration to us, exiles *malgré nous*, on our travels. In many ways he encapsulated the spirit in which, so we believed, the true Decadent should travel. Although the poet did little travelling himself, the image of the journey plays a seminal role in many of his poems. One of our favourites is *Le Voyage*. It is dedicated to Maxime du Camp, the photographer who accompanied Flaubert on his travels to Cairo (see chapter 4). Whenever we read this poem we felt as if he had looked into the very depths of our souls and seen there our own sad plight – a century and a half before! The poet writes:

> *Un matin nous partons, le cerveau plein de flamme*
> *Le coeur gros de rancune et de désirs amers,*
> *Et nous allons, suivant le rythme de la lame,*
> *Berçant notre infini sur le fini des mers:*

> One morning we leave, our minds aflame
> Our hearts swollen with rancour and bitter desires.
> We set off, following the rhythm of the oar
> Cradling our infinity on the finite sea.

There is little doubt that he foresaw precisely what we hoped our own travels might bring forth:

> *Etonnants voyageurs! quelles nobles histoires*
> *Nous lisons dans vos yeux profonds come les mers!*
> *Montre-nous les écrins de vos riches mémoires,*
> *Ces bijoux merveilleux, faits d'astres et d'éthers.*

> Astonishing travellers! What noble histories
> Do we read in your sea-deep eyes!
> Show us your casket filled with rich memories,
> Those marvellous jewels, made of stardust and ether.

In many ways Baudelaire was to play the role of Virgil to our Dante as we journeyed through the underworld of numerous cities. With this difference. Our travels could be described as an inversion of Dante's. Whereas the latter set out in search of spiritual love and enlightenment, we of course were only ever seeking out degradation and debauchery.

There is little doubt in our minds that the *Divine Comedy* is one of the most extraordinary travel books ever written, although one cannot help thinking that if Dante Alighieri were alive today and in the process of writing 'il suo poema', he would be leading us through an altogether different Inferno.

I suggest that those condemned to the first circle of this contemporary Hell would find themselves in the departure lounge at Gatwick airport, where shrieking infants are strapped into harnesses, boorish drunken louts lurch menacingly, husbands and wives are at each others throats with murderous intent, all are condemned to an eternity of delayed flights.

In the second circle they would be trapped in a renovated Tuscan farmhouse where the overweight host, a North London lawyer dressed in a ludicrous straw hat and brown ribbed socks, endlessly extols the virtues of a local wine which is only fit for clearing drains and forces it down the poor sinners' throats.

In the third circle, wretched souls are lashed to deck chairs beside the pool of a hotel in Barbados where they are surrounded by witless blonde harridans from Wilmslow with leathery skin who consider deep-fried camembert the height of sophistication and whose golf-playing husbands lie bloated and scarlet in the noon day sun.

The fourth circle is not a circle at all, but an endless narrow side street in a small Spanish coastal town. It is always four o'clock in the morning and lost souls, in search of a hotel that does not exist, are compelled to step over numberless bodies of pasty English youths who lie groaning in pools of their own vomit, watched over by their moronic bedraggled girlfriends.

The fifth circle resembles the Valley of the Malabolge, or 'evil wind'. Here sinners are buried up to their necks in the sand of a beach in Thailand, listening to a macrobiotic adolescent with a backpack reciting his vapid, self-obsessed verse while the tide of a shit-rich sea laps around their chins, threatening to engulf them.

In the sixth circle one tries in vain to escape from a bar crowded with enthusiastic yachtsmen. The seventh circle is my own personal hell. I sometimes wake with a start at night, bathed in sweat as I recall the horror. I am walking through the garrigue in Southern France. The heat is intense and I am surrounded by a chatty and lively group each carrying an easel under their arm. Yes, I am on a water-colouring holiday.

In the eighth circle the damned are forced for all eternity to take holiday snaps of coach parties of grotesquely obese Americans as they stand with their backs to the glorious west front of Chartres Cathedral and whine about the price of some vile trinket they have just bought.

The final most excruciating punishment is reserved for only the basest of humankind – the bigot, the sanctimonious and the pious. They will navigate the seas ceaselessly aboard that most grotesque Ship of Fools – a cross-channel ferry.

But let us return to Satan. The consequence of his first rebellion and what preceded his exile was a 'fall', and, as we never tire of pointing out, the word 'decadence' refers precisely to the act of falling, which puts me in mind of another of Baudelaire's great verses, *Icarus: the Fall*.

> *En vain j'ai voulu de l'espace*
> *Trouver la fin et le milieu;*
> *Sous je ne sais quel oeil de feu*
> *Je sens mon aile qui se casse.*

> In vain I sought out
> The end and the middle of space.
> Under the gaze of some fiery eye
> I felt my wing break apart.

My loudly professed admiration for Icarus – a man who was prepared to defy nature and the gods by attempting to fly – might go part of the way to explaining why I take such inordinate delight in air travel. In fact I have always maintained that, given the choice, the way I would prefer to die is in a plane crash. It is my fervent wish that the last few seconds of my life will be spent falling. I yearn to experience the sheer exhilaration and terror of those moments spent looking out over a vast expanse of earth, seeing the ground screaming up to greet me, then shattering my body to pieces. That would make my life complete. O Icarus, happiest of men! who in his moment of supreme failure must have experienced a moment of triumph like no other. Or, in Richard Le Gallienne's words:

*First drink the stars, then grunt amid the mire.*

Here is a death worthy of a Decadent. If one is to live decadently, one must surely be prepared to die decadently.

In order to pursue this interest of mine, I spent some time researching the locations of some of the most famous and spectacular air crashes in aviation history: Munich, New York, Mt. Fuji, Tenerife. I even produced a map of these sites and was intent on travelling, by way of pilgrimage, from one site to another. While in Japan, I commissioned a series of photographs to be taken of myself dressed as a Kamikaze pilot, and spent a week writing farewell poems in the traditional Kamikaze style.

*When the spring wind blows*
*Which are the blossoms that first touch the earth?*
*The pink cherry? The white cherry?*
*I am a petal of pink cherry blossom.*
*When I kiss the earth, do not lament.*

Later, when Medlar and I were travelling through Peru, I desperately wanted to visit the site in the Andes where several members of an Argentinian rugby team had crashed in a light aircraft and the survivors were reduced to slicing bits off their dead companions in order to avoid starvation. The allure of crash site and cannibalism was almost more than I could bear. Uncharacteristically, Medlar thought this was a little *de trop*. Try as I might to persuade him, he was deaf to my entreaties.

In general Medlar seems not to share my enthusiasm. Indeed he avoids flying whenever possible. He even turned down a lavish invitation to spend some time at the home of a Tampa millionairess on the grounds that:

'. . . *if God had meant us to fly, my dear, he would have given us all air miles. This has nothing to do with a fear of flying. Indeed, fear is an emotion which I relish and cultivate at every available opportunity. Rather, my aversion to air travel is due largely to my hatred of airports. For here one is confronted with the horror of contemporary travel in its most naked and strident form: the hordes of peasantry drifting like graz-ing bovines, the sense of utter futility in all human endeavour. All that ingenuity to master the air – the Brothers Wright, Sir Frank Whittle, Reginald 'Spitfire' Mitchell – and for what? The package tour! It is no coincidence that, apart from airports, the word 'terminal' is primarily associated with fatal diseases.'*

Medlar's preferred form of travel is the train, largely because he enjoys the florid architecture of railway stations and the opportunities they present for sexual misconduct. In this he hopes one day to emulate his great Uncle Walter who, at Avignon in 1855 among the temporary wooden buildings of the newly erected station, laid down a world standard for voyeurism which seems unlikely ever to be surpassed. (For the full sordid details, see the Appendix.) More importantly, there is something about the rhythm of trains which brings about a steep rise in the level of Medlar's libido. There was a period in his life when he was incapable of any sexual response anywhere except on a moving train. His favourite line was the light railway from Welshpool to Llanfair Caereinion. The following is an extract taken from a let-ter he wrote to me from a cheap Bed & Breakfast somewhere in the Welsh marches.

*'The train is pulled by a small steam engine – all busy little pistons and vertical thrusting smoke stack. It consists of four carriages which were made in Austria in the early 1920s at the death of the Austro-Hungarian empire. They were originally third class coaches with wooden slatted seats and the last coach was perfect for my purposes as it had an open-air observation platform at the back. From here I could look out over the undulating Welsh countryside and indulge at least three of my passions – copulating on a train, in the open air, with the additional stimulus of the fear of being detected. My orgasms have never been so protracted, nor have I produced such copious quantities of semen as I did during the course of those delightful journeys through the hills of mid Wales in the company of a local whore with the voices of*

*happy and excited schoolchildren ringing out from inside the little carriage.'*

Other forms of transport which we long considered worthy of the Decadent traveller include Cleopatra's barge ('*the poop whereof,*' according to Plutarch, *'was of gold, the sails of purple, and the oars of silver, which kept stroke in rowing after the sound of the music of flutes, oboes, citherns, viols and such other instruments as they played upon in the barge . . . out of the which there came a wonderful passing sweet savour of perfumes, that perfumed the wharf's side'*), a sea tractor with buoyant wheels, Napoleon's bath wagon (for a little touring holiday through central Europe), and Soraya Kashoggi's chocolate-filled private jet.

It was somewhat ironic that when we were forced to quit Edinburgh, Medlar and I were actually drawing up plans for our own ideal form of transport. This was a caravan. Or to be more precise, Raymond Roussel's motorised gypsy caravan.

Roussel was an immensely wealthy aesthete – you cannot help but admire a man who never wore the same shirt twice – and the writer of bizarre and wonderfully surrealistic novels such as *Impressions d'Afrique* and *Locus Solus.* He was also a rather reclusive man. Hence the caravan. We were intrigued by the following description of it which appeared in an edition of the *Revue du Touring Club de France.*

*So it is with the Sybarite in mind that we describe the very luxurious and practical house on wheels devised by M. Raymond Roussel. The author of* Impressions d'Afrique, *which is acclaimed by distinguished minds as a work of genius, has had built from his plans an automobile 30 feet long by 8 feet wide.*

*The car is really a small house. In fact it comprises, by means of an ingenious system: a sitting-room, a bedroom, a study, a bathroom, and even a small dormitory for the staff of three man-servants (two chauffeurs and a valet).*

*The bodywork by Lacoste is very elegant, and the interior both original and ingenious. To take two examples: the bedroom can in the daytime be turned either into a study or a sitting room, while the forward part (behind the driver's seat) at night turns into a little bedroom where the three man-servants can rest and wash (there is a basin in the panelling – to be seen to the left of the driver's seat).*

*The interior of M. Raymond Roussel's house comes from Maples.*

*There is electric heating and a paraffin stove. The hot water for the bath also runs on paraffin. The furniture is designed to cater for every need. There is even a Fichet safe. An excellent wireless set can pick up any European station.*

*This brief description gives some idea of how this remarkable villa on wheels – to which can be added a towable kitchen – affords its owner all the comforts of his own home on a scarcely reduced scale.*

*This luxurious installation is constructed on a Saurer chassis. On the flat its cruising speed is 25 mph. It can negotiate steep hills without fear thanks to an engine-braking system. It has a very tight turning circle which is very useful for twisting mountainous roads.*

*M. Raymond Roussel did not design and build his caravan – as he modestly calls it – as a mere whim, without intending to use it. As soon as it was built the caravan set off last year for a round trip of 2000 miles through Switzerland and Alsace. Every evening M. Roussel had a different view. He returned from his trip with incomparable impressions. This year at the start of the summer, he took to the road to follow his wandering fancy in search of constantly changing sensations.*

*It is to be hoped that the example of M. Raymond Roussel will be understood and followed by numerous sybarites and that the day will come when many houses on wheels will run on the world's roads, to the subtle satisfaction of their occupants.*

The most expensive form of travel we explored was space flight. As far as Medlar is concerned this is the ultimate fantasy for the Decadent traveller, although with the cost of a space suit running to about half a million dollars, I can only think that those astronauts must have frightfully good tailors.

Everyday details like the prohibitive cost of space-suits did not stop Medlar giving full vent to his astronautical fantasies in Cairo, where the sight of the pyramids unleashed a burst of prose so purple that one can almost smell the paper rotting beneath it. It is here that the unreality of Medlar's thinking reaches its apogee. The notion that we two professional lounge lizards (or 'salon iguanas' as we prefer to be known) might present ourselves for astronaut training is about as ludicrous a thought as the human brain is capable of formulating. It caused me no little distress when Medlar informed me that he had volunteered our services as Belgium's first men in space.

His fantasy is so all-consuming that he has elevated a genuine astronaut to the venerable company of Decadents. The victim of this improbable strategy is Michael Collins, a member of the Apollo XI crew that landed on the moon in July 1969. By some labyrinthine twist of logic, Medlar has designated this clean-cut American hero as a fellow-spirit of Wilde, Huysmans and Baudelaire.

Of course if one wants to be considered a truly Decadent travel-ler, the main impulse to resist is the desire to go somewhere in particular. This is absurd. The ideal state of mind for travelling is that of accidie, or apathetic torpor. This was the condition that the gods inflicted upon Ulysses after the Trojan War – which was why he spent so many years wandering aimlessly around the Mediterranean. Or perhaps a more poignant example closer to home is that of lone yachtsman Donald Crowhurst, whose voy-age began with single-minded fortitude and direction before degenerating into pointless wandering, insane fantasy and death. Not so much a lesson in how to travel, but rather in how to live one's life.

Here we are approaching the dark heart of what it is to travel decadently. In truth, those voyagers who have achieved immortality, whose names ring down the centuries – Sir John Mandeville, Marco Polo – probably never left home. The great Decadent journeys are those of the mind, and it is to Duc Jean Floressas des Esseintes – who else? – that we turn for the most refined and poignant account of one such journey. The account relates how the supreme dandy arrives in Paris, en route for London, and takes a cab for the Rue de Rivoli.

*Lulled by the monotonous beat of the rain drumming on his luggage and on the roof of the cab, like sacks of peas being tipped on his head, Des Esseintes began dreaming of his coming journey. The appalling weather seemed to him like a down payment of English life paid to him up front in Paris; and his mind conjured up an image of London as an immense sprawling rain-sodden metropolis stinking of soot and hot iron, constantly enveloped in a cloak of smog. In his mind he could see a line of dockyards stretching into the distance – cranes, capstans, and bales of merchandise, swarms of men – some perched on the masts and sitting astride the yardarms, while hundreds of others, their heads down and bottoms in the air, trundled cases along the quays and into the cellars.*

*All this activity was taking place in warehouses and on wharves washed by the dark, greasy waters of an imaginary river Thames, in the midst of a forest of masts, a tangle of beams and girders, piercing the pale, lowering clouds. Up above, trains sped past; and in the underground sewers, others rumbled along, occasionally letting out ghastly screams or spewing floods of smoke through the gaping mouths of air shafts. Meanwhile along every street, large or small, in an eternal twilight relieved only by the tawdry infamies of modern advertising, there flowed an endless stream of traffic between two columns of earnest, silent Londoners, trudging along with gaze fixed ahead and elbows glued to their sides.*

*Des Esseintes shuddered with delight at sensing himself lost in this fearful world of commerce, immersed in this isolating fog, engaged in this incessant activity, and trapped in this merciless machine which ground millions of poor wretches to dust . . .*

*But then the vision vanished as the cab suddenly jolted him up and down on the seat. . . .*

In the rue de Rivoli, Des Esseintes enters the Bodega and orders a glass of port.

*He was surrounded by swarms of English people. There were gangling clergymen, pale and clean-shaven, with round spectacles and greasy hair, dressed in black from head to foot – at one extremity soft hats, at the other laced shoes, and in between, incredibly long coats with little buttons running down the front. There were laymen with the bloated face of the pork butcher or the bulldog, apoplectic necks, ears like tomatoes, wine-coloured cheeks, stupid bloodshot eyes, and whiskery collars as worn by some of the great apes. At the far end of the wine-shop, a tow-haired man, as thin as a stick with white hairs sprouting from his chin like an artichoke, was using a magnifying glass to decipher the minute print of an English newspaper. . . .*

*Des Esseintes drifted into a reverie, conjuring up some of Dickens' characters, who were so partial to the rich red port he saw in glasses all about him, and used his imagination to people the cellar with a new set of customers – here was Mr Wickfield's white hair and ruddy complexion, there the sharp, blank features and emotionless eyes of Mr Tulkinghorn, the grim lawyer from Bleak House. These characters stepped right out of his memory to take their places in the Bodega, complete with all their mannerisms and gestures, for his recollection, revived by a recent reading of the novels, was extraordinarily precise and detailed. . . . He settled down comfortably in this London of the mind, happy to be indoors, and believing for a moment the dismal hooting of the tugs by the bridge behind the Tuileries was coming from boats on the Thames.*

Des Esseintes decides that he has enough time to dine before catching the train to Dieppe. He stops at a tavern where he eats the heartiest of meals: thick, greasy oxtail soup, smoked haddock, roast beef, blue stilton, rhubarb tart and a pint of porter. He observes the other inmates:

*As most of them turned their gaze upwards as they spoke, Des Esseintes concluded that almost all these Englishmen must be discussing the weather. Nobody laughed or smiled, and their suits matched their expressions: all of them were sombrely dressed in grey cheviot with nankin-yellow or blotting-paper-pink stripes. He cast an eye over his own clothes and was pleased to note that in colour and cut they did not differ appreciably from those worn by the people around him. He was delighted to realise that superficially at least he could claim to be a naturalized citizen of London.*

*. . .*

*Des Esseintes felt incapable of moving a muscle; a soothing feeling of warmth and fatigue was invading every limb, so that he could not even lift his hand to light a cigar.*

*'Get up and go, man,' he kept telling himself, but these orders were no*

*sooner issued than countermanded. After all, what was the good of moving, when a fellow could travel so magnificently sitting in a chair? Wasn't he already in London – whose smells, weather, citizens, food and even cutlery were all about him?*

. . .

*'When you come to think of it, I've seen and felt all that I wanted to see and feel. I've immersed myself in English life from the moment I left home. It would be insane to jeopardise such unforgettable experiences by a clumsy change of locality. As things are, I must have been suffering from some mental aberration to have thought of repudiating my old convictions, to have rejected the visions of my obedient imagination, and to have believed like any halfwit that it was necessary, interesting, and useful to travel abroad.'*

Alas! Not for us the unsullied delights of the imaginary voyage. For us it was all too real, and there is no disguising the fact that our period of exile was not a happy time for us, to such an extent that we were forced in the end to agree with Pascal of all people (hardly a prime candidate for the Decadent pantheon) when he said that *'Most of man's ills come from his being incapable of sitting quietly in his own drawing room.'* Or words to that effect.

As you will conclude if you venture any further into this dubious tome, Baudelaire's *Le Voyage* expresses our position with the greatest force and beauty.

> *Amer savoir, celui qu'on tire du voyage!*
> *Le monde, monotone et petit, aujourd'hui,*
> *Hier, demain, toujours, nous fait voir notre image:*
> *Une oasis d'horreur dans un désert d'ennui.*

> Oh bitter knowledge, which travel brings!
> The World, small and monotonous, today,
> Yesterday, tomorrow, always presents us with our own image:
> An oasis of horror in a desert of boredom!

Bitterness, boredom, horror . . . It is remarkable how quickly travel, widely regarded as one of life's chief pleasures, is transformed into a kind of hell in the crucible of the Decadent imagination.

Durian Gray
Mountcullen – August 1995

# SAINT PETERSBURG

I shall always think with affection of Finland – a gentle, gloomy country where I much enjoyed drinking Cloudberry brandy – it tastes like a mixture of cheap strawberry jam and silver polish – while being thrashed in a sauna with birch twigs before rolling naked in the snow. We bear our welts with pride.

Helsinki is obsessed with belly dancing and the tango. Medlar, who is such a passionate *tanguero,* was treated with reverence whenever he appeared on the dance floor. His tango is so immensely fiery, such a rush of jagged flame, that people can only stand back and be transfixed. Numerous couples had to slip out to the car park to cool off – and to satisfy the lust generated by his performance.

But we long ago realised that wherever we go, glamour and excitement follow. We are two rockets, scattering a trail of stars. Without our presence, there is little to detain the Decadent traveller in Finland. It is a land of tedium.

The journey to St Petersburg is no better: mile upon mile of regimented pine forest. It is quite remarkably monotonous – almost as bad as an evening of television – one feels absolutely like shooting oneself.

To relieve my boredom, I re-read Venedikt Yerofeev's *Moscow Stations.* A very fine book. It charts one of the great Decadent journeys of the 20th century. In geographical terms, Yerofeev does not travel very far – the short train ride from Moscow to Petushki. But in moral terms his journey is grandiose, an epic every bit as important as Dante's or Christ's walk to Golgotha. He moves from the torments of Kursk station, through the Purgatory of Kuchino and the dreamland of Kupavna, to a kingdom of mystical light in Petushki; from relative sanity and coherence into the pit of alcoholic degradation and madness, culminating in a surrealistically squalid death at the hands of strangers. My favourite part is the journey between Elektrougli and Kilometre 43. This shows the full force of Yerofeev's Decadent genius. Here he provides recipes for some of the most devastating cocktails ever to pass human lips.

He begins by taking a pledge: if he reaches Petushki in one piece he will create a cocktail which can be drunk without shame in the presence of God and man. He then goes on to display the breadth and profundity of his knowledge. Vodka by itself brings with it aggravation and a certain weariness of spirit. When mixed with eau-de-cologne it produces a degree of whimsy, but no pathos. Add a shot of methylated spirits and you end up with not only whimsy and pathos, but also metaphysics. This sublime triple cocktail – whimsical, pathetic, metaphysical – he calls Canaan Balsam.

He goes on to discuss other *chefs d'oeuvre* which his genius has given to the world – classics such as The Spirit of Geneva and Tears of a Komsomol Girl. But nothing prepares you for his final masterpiece. This is how he describes it:

*I now give you the last and the best. 'La fin couronne les oeuvres', as the poet said. In a word, I offer you Dog's Giblets, the drink that puts all others in the shade! It's not just a drink. It's the music of the spheres! What's the most beautiful thing in life? The struggle to free all mankind. But here's something even more beautiful – write it down:*

| | |
|---|---:|
| *Zhiguli beer* | *100g* |
| *Sadko the Wealthy Guest Shampoo* | *30g* |
| *Anti-dandruff solution* | *70g* |
| *Superglue* | *12g* |
| *Brake fluid* | *35g* |
| *Insecticide* | *20g* |

*Let it marinade for a week with some cigar tobacco, then serve.*

*I have incidentally received letters from idle readers recommending that the infusion thus obtained should be strained through a colander, no less. Yes, bung it into a colander and leave it overnight. God only knows what next – all these additions and emendations derive from a flabby imagination and a lack of vision. That's where these absurd notions come from.*

*Anyway, your Dog's Giblets is served. Drink it in big gulps when the first stars appear. After two glasses of this, I tell you, a person becomes so inspired that you can walk up to within five feet of them and spit right in their moosh for a whole half-hour, and they won't utter a word.*

Re-reading these recipes brought tears to my eyes. We used to serve these cocktails at the Decadent. Indeed the memory of the incisive odour of brake fluid and shampoo fills my nostrils with Proustian intensity as I write . . .

As the train crossed the frontier into Mother Russia from Karelia we sensed we were approaching something like the Heart of Darkness. The rows of pines were interspersed now with areas of desolate scrubland, each one grotesquely ornamented with a huge, deserted, crumbling factory. They stood there like hideous parodies of medieval ruins. Every now and then, as the train trundled past, one would catch sight of figures moving furtively amid the decrepit edifices, and it became clear that, far from being abandoned, these factories were still functioning. It was as if one had come across a community of monks, ragged and starving, still inhabiting the skeletons of their monastic buildings.

As we approached St Petersburg, our excitement and anticipation began to soar. The city held out the promise of Decadence on a colossal scale. The moment was perfect. The Soviet empire was crumbling by the day. There was no one, not even on the horizon, with the strength or will to arrest its decline. Only an ever-growing band of criminals, perverts and madmen picking over the pieces of the rotting carcass. Vice and corruption reigned supreme. We were approaching the very Republic of Decadence – the Last Days of Rome – the empurpled corpse of a rotting Byzantium.

As we stepped from the train, our first impressions did not disappoint. Everyone on the platform – passengers, porters, station officials, beggars, food-sellers, whores – seemed drunk, quite possibly on Dog's Giblets. There was a glittering savagery in the air, a kind of compressed explosive charge, as if all the buried corruption and violence of the city's past was about to erupt from beneath its streets.

This gave way to another impression as we left the station. What shall I call it? Entropy? Accidie? Weltschmerz? 'Dissolution has seeped into its very stones,' sighed Medlar, as we glanced out of the taxi window at the endless, rain-soaked 18th century façades that flashed past. 'I feel sure it's all about to collapse into the mire.'

St Petersburg, very much like Medlar and I, was Decadent from birth. The site where Peter the Great chose to build a new capital was a miserable, uninhabited island among the swamps at the mouth of the river Neva. Combined with the personality of its founder – tyrannical, unpredictable, needlessly cruel, a keen and sadistic amateur dentist – is it at all surprising that St Petersburg attracted us so mesmerically?

'The foundations of Petersburg rest on tears and corpses,' wrote the historian, Nikolai Karamzin. And here is Vassily Kluychevsky:

*I doubt one could find any battle in military history that brought about the death of more soldiers than the number of labourers who died in Petersburg. . . . Peter called his new capital his paradise, but for the people it turned out to be nothing more than a huge graveyard.*

It was not just the common labourers who were sacrificed on the altar of Peter's grandiose vision. Alexandre Le Blond, the architect who was responsible for the overall plan of the city, died after a beating from the Tsar who was displeased over a minor detail.

Among the most impressive of the early buildings was the palace of Prince Menshikov which stood on Vasilyevsky Island. Here Peter was regularly entertained in a dining room where around the walls stood tables each large enough to support a whole roast bull.

The cabaret at such evenings was noteworthy. What it lacked in sophistication it made up for in exuberance. A fat court jester would ride around the room on a small horse and every time Tsar Peter drained his goblet, the jester would pull out a pistol and fire a shot into the ceiling. This shot however was merely the signal for a deafening cannonade to be set off on the embankment. It was claimed that when Prince Menshikov was throwing a party, more gunpowder was used up than in the storming of a Tartar fortress.

Another of Peter's party favourites was enormous pies. He was particularly delighted when a beautiful, semi-naked female midget draped in red ribbons burst out through the crust. He kept large numbers of dwarfs, jesters, acrobats and monsters for similar entertainments.

Peter was a great dancer. It gave him the opportunity to inflict pain on members of the old Russian aristocracy, the Boyars. Aged, venerable and deeply traditional, they were characterised by their long grey beards, which the Tsar made them shave off, just to humiliate them. He also forced them to take part in energetic western dances like the jig. He was particularly delighted by the intense pain this caused to any of the old Boyars who happened to be suffering from gout.

No one dared leave the festivities without Peter's permission. Foreign ambassadors often simply fell asleep on the floor. Then Peter would hold a candle over them while other guests urinated on them.

The next morning, guests would retire to one of St Petersburg's thirty or so bathhouses. These were located on the riverbank. The revellers would get undressed in the street, enter the bathhouse and steam themselves until the heat was unbearable. Then they would run outside and jump into the river. In the winter, when the river was frozen, the figure of the Tsar, looking like an enormous cooked lobster, could be seen cavorting in the snow.

One particularly fine example of Peter the Great's fun-loving nature comes from Pushkin's *Table Talk*:

*Once a little Negro servant who accompanied Peter on a walk squatted to evacuate his bowels and suddenly cried out in terror. 'Sire! Sire! My guts are coming out!' Peter approached and examined him saying: 'Don't give me that! It's not your guts. It's a tape worm!'*

*And he pulled the tapeworm out with his fingers.*

Hot on the heels of Tsar Peter came another extraordinary Decadent – Catherine the Great. In all she ruled Russia for 34 years, during which time, blood, robbery, rape, '. . . everything,' according to Helvetius, 'became legitimate and even virtuous for the public welfare.'

She had come to rule Russia through her marriage to the heir, Grand Duke Peter Federovitch. The Grand Duke, despite his aristocratic pedigree, was in many ways a very modern husband. He trained dogs in his bedroom, played with toy soldiers, went to bed in his clothes and boots, and caressed dolls in preference to his wife.

The unconsummated marriage provoked the Grand Duke's mother, the Empress Elisabeth, to threaten a medical examination in order to ascertain the fertility of the couple. The Grand Duke was furious and in retaliation took a mistress who was both ugly and a hunchback. He enjoyed waking Catherine at night by punching her in the ribs and telling her how much he preferred his hunchback to her.

After ten years of marriage and two miscarriages Catherine provided an heir and was promptly ignored by everyone at court. She took to reading the *philosophes* and the pursuit of self-gratification. An ambassador at that time reported:

*It was a custom in Russia to regard the Empress's bed as a place of pleasure which could be reached easily; one was allowed to aspire to it freely and it was even a mark of good taste to show that it was desired.*

When his mother the Empress Elisabeth died in 1760, Grand Duke Peter mourned her passing by presiding over an orgy in the room next to the one where her body lay in state. His mistress, variously described as fat, vulgar and evil-smelling, now reigned at court where she was much given to drinking and swearing like a soldier. However, Catherine had rather different ideas about the succession. A coup d'état deposed Peter and brought Catherine to the throne. The Grand Duke was finally murdered at Ropcha, almost certainly on the orders of his wife, who had by now developed some highly innovative feminist principles.

In the absence of her husband, the Empress Catherine set about providing herself with a steady stream of lovers to satisfy her sexual appetite. One of her great favourites was Count Grigory Orlov – much in demand among the maids of honour at the Empress' court.

The name Orlov was of course well-known to us from our restaurant days. One of our favourite chefs, Urbain Dubois, worked for Prince Nikolai Orlov, nephew to the prodigious Grigory, and created the dish known as 'Veal Orlov' in his honour.

In homage to our beloved Urbain, we made a journey to the Gatchina Palace, 45 kilometres south west of St Petersburg, a property which was granted to Orlov by a grateful and thoroughly satisfied monarch. Orlov recorded his prowess with erotic frescoes and furniture. We knew of these from a series of grainy sepia photographs probably taken just after the First World War. The furniture comprised a large round mahogany dining table – supported by four thick legs in the form of enormous ejaculating penises, which are in turn supported on four wooden feet. At first sight these feet have the appearance of testicles, but on closer inspection they prove to be breasts. The top of the table is deep, which has allowed for a series of drawers to be set into it. The handles for the drawers are made in the form of the torso of a squatting woman seen from the back. The handle is grasped by inserting the fingers between the buttocks of the torso and pulling. A most satisfactory and efficient design. One would not have thought that opening and shutting a drawer could be such a pleasurable experience.

In addition to the table there was a set of very fine dining chairs, each ornately decorated with exquisite carvings. Just below the seat at the front, for example, is to be found a carving of a woman lying on her back with her legs wide apart. At the top of the backrest was a carving of a young woman with a penis in her mouth. On others is portrayed a devil licking a vagina. The arms consisted of two figures: a naked woman along the upper part, with a satyr below inserting his fingers into her quim. Another group at the top of an armchair comprises two naked women masturbating and fellating a satyr. Due to the age of the photographs it is difficult to assess accurately the quality of the carving. The maker was no Grinling Gibbons evidently. However this lack is more than made up for by the exuberance of the subjects.

The room in which the furniture was designed to stand had been decorated with frescoes, equally explicit in nature. Young women with long flowing hair and proportions reminiscent of Rubens or Boucher are shown being penetrated by enormously well-endowed satyrs in every conceivable sexual position. Curiously, many of the women have a rather 1920s look about the face – Clara Bow lips and heavy dark eyelashes.

Unfortunately our pilgrimage was in vain. The furniture had long since disappeared – looted from the palace by German soldiers during the Second World War. It may now grace some vast and gloomy Bavarian schloss, or perhaps an industrialist's villa in the outskirts of Dusseldorf, but I suspect it may have ended up on Hermann Goering's yacht, where the podgy lothario liked to entertain guests to a hunter's dinner of schnapps and raw stag's testicles before planning the next day's raids on Coventry or Birmingham.

Count Orlov was eventually repudiated by Catherine for his infidelities. Imprisoned for a time in Gatchina, he ended his days wandering aimlessly through Europe. He married his nineteen year old cousin and died insane. Truly, a fine end to a glorious existence! Orlov provides us all with a shining example of the Great Life.

After the departure of Orlov, it was left to Potemkine to act as the Empress's pimp, procuring lovers according to a specific set of criteria, namely, they must be without political ambition, cultured and good conversationalists, and gifted with boundless sexual energy. They also had to undergo an entrance exam, so to speak. The Empress would stand in a darkened drawing room and was introduced to the elected who could not tell who was there. He had to show what he was made of and was accepted or rejected accordingly. Six were kept in the entourage during the last two decades of her life. At the age of over sixty, the Empress was being serviced by a man of twenty years old. To vary her diet, she would occasionally review her regiment of guards and choose a simple soldier to share her bed. Her choice was determined by the size of his nose. The guard would spend one night in the arms of the Empress and was executed the following day. Catherine died as we would all wish to – attempting to make love to a stallion.

It is difficult to imagine when she had the time or the energy to devote to the commissioning of buildings. Yet somehow she did, as the enormous number of her palaces around St Petersburg testifies. In one of her letters she explained her approach:

*Our storm of construction now rages more than ever before, and it is unlikely that an earthquake could destroy as many buildings as we are erecting. Construction is a sort of devilry, devouring a pile of money, and the more you build the more you want to build. It's simply a disease, something like a drinking fit . . .*

Of all the great architectural projects undertaken by Catherine, one, for us, stands out: the Sledding Hill Pavilion at the Oranienbaum. This was intended for ice sledding in winter and roller coasting in summer. It was essentially a set of wooden hills inside a rococo pavilion. It comprised a series of elaborately terraced stairs, with pastel blue and white exteriors capped by a bell-shaped cupola. A highly ornate and ludicrously expensive building designed entirely for frivolity.

For some, mid-winter is not the best time for visiting St Petersburg. For us it was ideal. We went for weeks without seeing daylight, living in darkness, which is the true Decadent element. Without the distraction of fact and detail – so garishly intrusive by day – the imagination is free to unfold its fetid wings. How often we stood on Nevsky Prospect and recreated the intensity of Gogol's reaction:

*Oh don't put any trust in Nevsky Prospect! . . . It's all deception and dreams, it's not what it appears to be! . . . For God's sake, keep away from the street lamp! And walk as quickly as you can. You'll be lucky if you escape with nothing worse than a drop of its foul-smelling oil on your elegant coat. Everything else besides the street lamp exhales deceit. It lies all the time, that Nevsky Prospect, but especially when night settles on it, separating the white and pale walls of the houses, when the entire city is transformed into thunder and sparkle, myriads of carriages falling from the bridges, postilions shouting and leaping onto horses, and when the devil himself lights the lamps for no other reason than to show things in their unreal form.*

And how well we understood Grigoryev! Even though he was describing the 'white nights' of the city, when the sun never sets, we found it much easier to visualize than if we had simply seen it.

*And in those hours when my proud city*
*Is covered by night without dark and shadow*
*When everything is transparent, then a swarm of disgusting visions*
*Flickers before me . . .*
*Let the night be as clear as day, let everything be still,*
*Let everything be transparent and calm -*
*In that calm an evil illness lurks -*
*And that is the transparency of a suppurating ulcer.*

Voznesensky Prospect at night is one of the finest things on earth. We often strolled it after dinner, smiling graciously at the expensive prostitutes, avoiding the drunks as they brawled clumsily in doorways, stepping gingerly over the unconscious lying stretched out on the pavement outside the elegant entrances to cramped and squalid apartments . . . As we did so, we knew that such scenes had been played out many times before in the history of the city. The true beauty of St Petersburg lies in the fact that nothing ever changes.

For us, of course, any notion of progress or the perfectability of man is totally abhorrent. There may have been a few brief moments in the history of Petersburg when it appeared that progress was being made, but in fact this has proved illusory. And the inhabitants of the city itself have always been aware of this quality. As Prince Vayazemsky wrote at the beginning of the 19th century:

*' . . . Petersburg can serve as an emblem for our life . . . In people you can't tell Ivan from Peter; in time you can't distinguish between today and tomorrow; everything is the same.'*

The sordidness we witnessed returned us immediately to the 1850s. Alexander II had just freed the serfs and consequently they invaded St Petersburg in waves, just as the flood waters of the Neva had risen so many times to engulf the city. Every vice known to man began to flourish in the poverty they brought with them. Prostitutes were not only drawn from the ranks of the peasantry, but many were the wives and daughters of soldiers or retired clerks. Even high-born mothers were prepared to sell their daughters into depravity, out of oppressive poverty. Much of this economic activity centred on the Haymarket, which was a gathering place for hawkers, thieves, conmen and tricksters of all sorts. If you bought a pie in the Haymarket more often than not its filling would be nothing more than a filthy old rag. Any complaint would be met with 'What do you expect for three kopeks? Velvet?'

And now, with the collapse of the Communist system – a second freeing of the serfs – all Hell has broken loose again. Anything and anybody can be bought here. Anything from a murderer's bullet to a nuclear warhead, from a politician to a rent boy, from the best caviar to the brain of a Kazakhstan pig. In Petersburg, Life and Death are for sale. Neither is particularly expensive. This is why we feel so at home here.

Nowadays, the purveyors of these goods and services are of course the Mafiya. We had a memorable meeting with one of their number in the restaurant of the Astoria hotel. The first thing we noticed was that the occupants of several tables in one corner of the restaurant were being moved by the serving staff, hurriedly and unapologetically, to a distant part of the restaurant . The guests were even compelled to carry their own plates from one table to another. We were delighted. This was exactly the sort of behaviour we used to encourage at the Decadent Restaurant. But there it was done for the sheer hell of it. Here there was a purpose, which became clear when, a few minutes later, an entourage of dark-suited men appeared. They looked as if they had been taking lessons in deportment from the Kray Brothers. They even held their cigarettes cupped in the palm of their hands. In the middle of this ring of menace, and almost hidden by it, strode a very short, very fat, savage-looking man wearing a very nasty designer track suit. He was playing with a set of car keys in the same manner that Greek men play with their worry beads. (The keys were the outward sign of inward vice. We had seen similar Mercedes keys dangling from similarly chubby fingers in the cemeteries of St Petersburg. There, however, they were made of stone, part of the fabulously kitsch life-size statues which stand atop the tombs of the victims of Mafiya contract killings.

We cannot speak too highly of such unabashed vulgarity). The group of men made their way across the restaurant in complete silence, broken only by the rattling of these keys. After the underside of the tables had been thoroughly checked, the boss sat down and a phalanx of jittery waiters fussed about him.

In the event, once he had been informed that we were the former owners of the world-renowned Decadent Restaurant, the *'reketiry'* (racketeer) invited us to join him. This was not an invitation to refuse. No sooner had we sat down than we were discussing the possibility of opening a new Decadent Restaurant in St Petersburg. For some reason the deal seemed to turn on us purchasing three tons of enriched plutonium. Despite the excellent price, we felt obliged to decline, as we had nowhere to keep it. The *reketiry* was clearly disappointed. Still, he remained quite civil and asked us if we required any automatic weapons, armoured limousines, passports or other merchandise. 'How about two tickets to the Mariinsky Theatre tonight?' we asked.

One of the minders was immediately despatched and had returned with tickets before the dessert arrived. We parted on the best of terms and the Mafiya boss told us if we ever wanted anybody killed we were to come to him. It would cost no more than the price of two hundred cigarettes.

Of all the buildings we visited in St Petersburg, we felt that the Mariinsky Theatre best encapsulated the Decadence of the city. It has a magnificent façade, and in the auditorium everything is gilded wood and ostentatious stucco. But behind the scenes, backstage, the conditions are cramped and unspeakably filthy. I find it irresistible. Nowhere do brilliance and squalor, opulence and degradation, beauty and ugliness exist in such close proximity. Side by side sit the elegance of high eighteenth century culture and the baseness of medieval life. I noted for example that there are only three toilets available for a corps de ballet of 450 dancers. I swear that if you are foolish enough to inhale while relieving yourself, death follows almost instantaneously.

I am sometimes asked what I was doing inspecting the sanitary arrangements backstage at the Mariinsky. To this naïve question I invariably reply that I am a member of an international body of volunteers who travel the world evaluating public lavatories; I add that the work is entirely unpaid and carried out purely for the sake of international cleanliness. Anyone stupid enough to ask the question in the first place is usually impressed. Occasionally they offer to give money to this noble organization. Not wishing to hurt their feelings, I allow them to make a donation.

It was during one of my charitable backstage forays that I met Elena Serdukov, a member of the Kirov corps de ballet. Ah, quelle danseuse! A woman of infinite suppleness! I remember spending hours sitting in a musty armchair in her tiny flat, which was crowded with cheap china and glass knick-knacks of all sorts, just watching her pleasure herself with her own foot.

It was with Elena that I made my weekend journey to Siberia – an episode which severely tested my friendship with Medlar. Painful as it is to recall, I feel I must set it down in all its excruciating detail – not least for the sake of posterity.

The first leg of this journey was by plane from Petersburg to Novosibirsk. I was particularly looking forward to this, because air travel in Russia is about the most dangerous anywhere in the world. The odds of dying in a Russian airliner have been calculated at seven times the global average. During one 18 month period, more than a dozen planes, commercial and military, crashed in the former Soviet Union, killing a total of more than 500 people. The reasons are the time-honoured ones in Russia – drunkenness, incompetence and corruption – and one recent and notable case of human error, when the pilot allowed his teenage son to take the controls of an Airbus A-310. The crash killed all 75 people on board.

Alas, the trip was uneventful. We landed safely in Novosibirsk, took a dilapidated taxi into town and arrived at the railway station in time to board the afternoon train to Akademgorodok.

Elena and I found a quiet compartment, where wrapped in black bear furs and insulated against the cold by large quantities of bison grass vodka, we whiled away the journey in innocent and carefree gamahuchage.

We reached the city of Akademgorodok by early evening. The spring sun was setting, casting a feeble, livid light on a large, crumbling white office block opposite the station. This was my first glimpse of the shining city of Soviet Science.

What can I say about Akademgorodok? Well, it's a shithole. A decaying shithole. It was a project approved by Krushchev in the late 1950s. Its conception was grandiose and overweening. A city of 200,000 scientists, technicians and their families would rise from the midst of virgin Siberian forest. A score of research institutes would be created there, each one a leader in world science, proving yet again the superiority of Socialist principles over an effete and decadent West. Needless to say, in true Russian spirit, the whole place was a disaster from the outset. Ineptitude and stupidity on a monumental scale characterised its construcion. It did not occur to the planners, for example, that in a region where the temperature falls to minus fifty centigrade, special materials might be required. The nuclear power station there was built by teams of unskilled drunkards. It began to fall apart even before it was finished. By the time we arrived, there was no money to pay wages, food was scarce and the telephone lines had been cut. Starvation, depression and suicides were commonplace.

'More than fifty people kill themselves each week here,' Elena informed me. She is the purveyor of some fascinating statistics and she has a mode of delivery which makes them sound like obscene poetry. 'It's worst during the Spring. Almost as if, having survived the winter, they have no strength left.'

The first, indelible impression one gains of the city is the contrast between the ideal of its original foundation and the squalor of its present state. It imbues the place with a rare beauty. However, this is all rather tangential to the main reason for my visit, or – as I liked to think of it – my quest.

I had come to this city because Elena happened to mention that her brother was a medical technician in one of its Institutes. In itself this was of no interest to me. But she went on to say that he had come up with a novel way of making a little foreign capital, with which he managed to supplement his diet of root vegetables – he hired out endoscopy equipment.

We stood outside the station for some time before deciding that neither a taxi nor a bus was going to come our way. So Elena and I set off across a snow-covered piece of waste ground, which may have been a public park at one time, towards one of a series of identical white blockhouses. We entered an empty reception area. There was nobody about. An air of abandonment haunted the place. Naively I headed for the lift. Elena told me there was no point and steered me up two flights of crumbling concrete steps, to the end of an anonymous corridor. Facing us was a door. Elena knocked gently three times and I followed her in.

The room we entered was white-tiled and brightly-lit, with a high examination bed in the middle. The bed was covered in a grubby sheet. I was introduced to Elena's brother, the medical technician. We quickly concluded a business transaction, drank each other's health in surgical spirit and he left. Apparently he needed to switch off some equipment in the intensive care unit to make sure we had enough power.

Elena invited me to lie face down on the bed. When I was comfortably positioned she wheeled a television monitor on a trolley in front of me. Then she turned out the lights, so that the room was filled with the glow from the monitor. She deftly removed my trousers so that my arse – which might be described as the 'Portal' or 'Threshold' to this uncommon voyage – was now exposed to the almost sub-zero temperature of the room. The cold made it more than a little difficult for her to insert the small metal probe she had in her hand. At each touch of the icy steel instrument, my rectal muscle contracted like a frightened sea anemone. On several occasions I watched on the monitor as the dildo-like instrument approached my arsehole only for the screen to go dark and impenetrable. It was only by virtue of Elena's gentle touch and warm tongue that it was persuaded to relax sufficiently for her to insert the probe. I felt a momentary stab of pain which diverted my attention from the screen and when I looked again it had gone black. I was on the point of cursing the incompetence of Soviet technology when the screen began to give off a dark red glow. A picture slowly emerged as the camera moved onwards and upwards. The images it sent back were breath-taking. This is the sort of journey every true Decadent should make at least once in their life. By that I mean the Journey into the Interior. I watched fascinated as I wandered slowly along the strange pulsating alleyways of my own body, along the eerie passages and living tunnels of my inner world. Corridors of tissue twist and curve in endless contortions. The colours – the sombre browns, the vivid reds and fuchsia-pinks – are utterly extraordinary. They glisten and shift in endless variety. It was quite unlike any voyage of discovery I had ever made before. And with a Kirov ballerina as the tour guide!

Looking back on it, the closest I could think of in terms of comparison was the autumnal afternoon I spent drifting in Count Magnafiga's balotina through the narrow canals of Dorsoduro in Venice while being gently and surreptitiously sodomised by his manservant, Marcello.

The moments of greatest excitement arrived when it was necessary to make a decision about which course to choose wherever a bifurcation presented itself. At one such point I was seized with a sudden attack of panic, terrified by the notion that this voyage might stretch out to eternity and I would never find my way out. Elena had to spend some time calming me before she continued her probing. After that, the journey had a wonderfully soporific and languid effect upon my spirit.

I don't know how long it was before Elena removed the probe, but by then I was experiencing an immense and overwhelming fatigue. In this state of weary elation, Elena helped me back to the train station and we returned to Novosibirsk, where we found a grubby modern hotel to spend the night. However, I was so emotionally exhausted that the surroundings failed to impinge upon me in any way.

When we returned to St Petersburg I was reunited with Medlar, who was more furious than I have ever seen him. He stormed around the hotel bedroom shouting imprecations, accusing me of deserting him in favour of an acrobatic whore. He was under the illusion that I had simply gone off for a dirty weekend with the ballerina. When I told him the real reason for the trip he calmed down a bit.

'At least I can understand why you did it,' he said. 'Even if I cannot forgive you.'

When the true extent of what he had missed finally dawned on him, Medlar was even less ready to forgive me. For no reason other than perversity, he started quibbling about the cost. How could I have gone all that distance just to have a television camera stuffed up my arse?

'That was the whole point,' I replied. 'The very futility of it.'

Poor Medlar. When he gets upset like that, he seems to lose his capacity to think straight.

# NAPLES

Virgilio is the owner of a bookshop in the Via San Pietro a Majella.

I first met him in the bar at the Kirov Ballet in St Petersburg, while waiting for Durian to return from Akademgorodok and his 'journey to the interior'. I was expatiating on the difficulty of finding any genuinely Decadent cities. A number of names sprang to mind: Las Vegas of course, Rome, Berlin, New York, and so on, but we had come to the realization that we wanted something different: corruption, yes, but without its train of sycophancy, stupidity and designer shops; we were in search of that elusive thing, a place of squalor and magnificence in equal measure – both, if possible, to be seized in a single electrifying moment, a white-hot thunderflash of aesthetic intensity which would fuse us with its *genius loci* in a cataclysm of obliterating fire . . . Virgilio, who had listened to this vodka-fuelled rant with a kind of amused tolerance, presented his card and suggested a visit to Naples.

I could not wait to tell Durian of my plan to move on. Firstly I hoped that by leaving St Petersburg, he would be released from the baleful influence of the dancing tart, and secondly, I was hoping that our visit might coincide with one of the notorious Neapolitan festivals which the Marquis de Sade describes in his *Voyages d'Italie*. De Sade writes:

*Events open with a feast – the most barbaric spectacle you could possibly imagine. On a huge scaffold which has been decorated in the rustic manner, a large quantity of meats are displayed in such a way that they constitute part of the decoration. Among them, brutally cruci-fied, hang geese, chickens and turkeys which, suspended live by two or three nails, amuse the populace with their writhing motions, until the time comes for the whole display to be looted. Loaves of bread, dried cod, sides of beef, sheep graze in areas of the decor which represent a field guarded by cut-out men finely attired. Lengths of material are arranged in such a way as to form a billowing sea on which floats a vessel loaded with food or furniture in the local style. Such is the arrangement (often very tasteful) of this bait, dangled in front of a savage populace in order to excite or rather perpetuate its voracious greed and love of stealing. For, having seen this spectacular display, it would be difficult not to conclude that this is more a training ground for looters than a true feast.*

*On the appointed day at midday, and following a signal from the king, the people rush forward and in the twinkling of an eye everything has been carried off, ripped to shreds and pillaged with indescribable frenzy. The first time I observed this terrifying scene it reminded me of the fleshing of stag hounds. And it often has tragic consequences . . . I witnessed a moment of such horror it made my hair stand on end. Two men attacked each other over a slab of beef. . . . Immediately the knives were out. In Naples and Rome this is the only way that an argument is settled. One of the men fell, drowning in his own blood. But the victor did not enjoy his triumph for long. The ladder he was climbing to claim his prize gave way under him. Clinging on to the side of beef, he fell on top of the corpse of his rival. Wounded, dead, it's all the same. All you could see was a bloody mass. Then other contestants, taking advantage of the failure of the two men, swooped to extricate the meat from under the corpses and carry it off in triumph still dripping with the blood of the rivals.*

Such an event, I had always felt, would have gone down magnificently in Edinburgh as a way of promoting the Decadent Restaurant. We could have transformed the entire Royal Mile into a large *Raft of the Medusa* – but Durian was against the idea. He thought it too tame, and suggested that we leave that kind of thing to the National Trust.

This scene of barbarity was not the only thing to upset the Divine Marquis. He describes Naples as a place where the climate, the food and an all-pervasive corruption are constant invitations to debauchery.

*It is physically impossible to imagine the extent to which debauchery has been pushed here.*

*The streets by night are full of the most unfortunate women, offered up as victims to the brutality of all and sundry; women who for the most meagre sum will incite you to every conceivable form of licentiousness, even those which, by virtue of their sex, they should abhor.*

*How one sighs to see children of the tenderest age and even those in whom the faculty of reason is not yet formed, share with their mothers and their sisters the infamy of this awful corruption! In all truth I can say that in Naples I have seen little girls of four or five offer to satisfy the basest of desires and, when one succumbs to their temptations, they even ask that one perform that most unnatural of acts as, due to their age, they are not yet capable of indulging in the normal practice which the Creator has ordained for those of their sex.*

*This would be as nothing if that were as far as it went, but these same horrors are offered to you by the sex which should find depravity repellent. In Naples, both men and women are in competition with each other to excite the passions. Even in your own home you are not safe. A mother will offer you any of her children, male or female, whichever will most satisfy your desires. A sister will offer her brother, a father his daughter, a husband his wife. It is simply a question of paying. With enough money in Naples you could have a duchess of the highest rank.*

As if all this were not reason enough to visit Naples, I had long wanted to visit the city which had been home to that intriguing couple – Sir William and Lady Hamilton.

History has grossly misrepresented Emma Hamilton. Far from being a beautiful and tragic protagonist in one of the grandest adulteries since Tristan and Isolde, she was in fact a grotesquely overweight and immensely common whore. By the age of 14 she was a prostitute in London and was soon taking part in sex shows. Her accent was on the cheap side of Cheapside. When she was 'collected' by Sir William he was quite happy to turn a blind eye to her various liaisons, especially with the dreary seaman who made a career out of having bits of himself shot off – a sort of elective amputation I have always thought. She was obviously deeply attracted to seamen, and her obesity – the Comtesse de Courville on seeing her for the first time was heard to exclaim 'My God, what a whopper!' – proved a very effective way of concealing several illicit pregnancies. And in her political views, she would have made Mussolini sound like a bleeding heart liberal. She has long held a cherished place in my trousseau.

And so we flew out of the still wintry city of Peter the Great and headed south, gliding in over that tremendous blue bay in an ancient Tupolev, overhead lockers rattling, stewardesses clenching their pale thighs in high-heeled terror, while Vesuvius beckoned in the morning sunlight and our souls quivered with expectation.

We found Virgilio's bookshop without trouble. I say without trouble, but that is not strictly true. At the airport we approached five different taxi drivers and showed them the address. The first three shook their heads. The fourth simply spat into the dust at our feet, which we took to be a peculiarly Neapolitan way of saying no. The fifth taxi driver grinned at us lasciviously, clutched his genitalia enthusiastically and ushered us into his cab.

We were dropped off in a particularly dingy backstreet just west of the cathedral of San Gennaro. As we walked down this narrow street between the tall tenements, I could not help noticing the very strange manner in which Durian was behaving. He kept looking up, nervously eyeing the decrepit balconies linked by lines of washing above our heads. His behaviour finally irritated me so much that I asked him to explain himself. He said that he was looking out for falling pigs. This explanation I felt was insufficient. He continued. Ever since reading the Graham Greene story about an Englishman in Naples who is crushed to death by a pig falling from a balcony on which it was being fattened, he had dreaded finding himself in a similar nightmarish scenario.

I found this anxiety of Durian's totally comprehensible. Given that I had spent three years in the Christian Brothers seminary at Maynooth, I knew only too well what it was like to be pinned to the floor under the weight of some grunting, malodorous, pink creature.

We eventually found Virgilio's bookshop situated discreetly between a shop selling religious paraphernalia – statues of saints with martyred flesh and pious eyes looking out from under hooded eyelids – and a shoemender's. From the outside, the bookshop looked reputable enough and as I went inside there was nothing about the interior to disabuse me of this impression. Like all small bookshops it was small, dark and full of books. However, it did also contain more than its fair share of strikingly beautiful young males. They turned in our direction as we stood in the doorway.

'We seek Virgilio,' I announced imperiously. An olive-skinned youth with sunglasses pushed up on top of his head approached us and asked the nature of our business.

'We are friends of his. He has invited us to come and stay. I am Medlar Lucan and this is Durian Gray. Need we say more?'

'Yes.'

'Ah. Well, we once ran a restaurant in Edinburgh – The Decadent. You may have heard of *that*.'

'No.'

This response surprised and disappointed me in equal measure. I had always assumed that the name of the Decadent resounded throughout the civilised world. The young man was scrutinising us suspiciously.

'You are with the Catholic Church, perhaps?'

I spluttered in disbelief. 'My dear boy, do I *look* as if I am with the Catholic Church?'

He glanced at my Hardy Amies suit, which I had paired for the day with a gold and turquoise Hawaiian shirt with 'Greetings from Honolulu!' scrawled in pink copperplate among the palm trees, together with some exceedingly rare open-toed purple ostrich-skin golfing shoes by Hermann of Prague . . . But before he could articulate the complex feelings that were running like savannah fires through his exquisitely shaped head, our host appeared from the back of the shop. Virgilio exchanged a few words with the excitable youth who walked off to join his friends. He welcomed us heartily and asked us to forgive Salvatore (the name of the gorgeous young man) explaining that he was suspicious of all strangers ever since the bookshop had become the target of attacks by some of the more fanatical members of Opus Dei. But, he went on, this was not something we needed to concern ourselves with. Instead, over a ferocious little cup of espresso, he launched into a eulogy of his home town.

'Napoli! Birthplace of Frankenstein, centre of the occult, shrine of alchemy, South Pole of the Knights Templar, volcanic, unstable, majestic in its climate and crime-rate, the home of everything that is cheap, noisy, decaying, deliquescent ... Poised on the lip of extinction, this sunlit gateway to the underworld purrs like a cat on a witches' cauldron ... Pozzuoli, Lake Avernus, Solfatara, Vesuvius, the city rests on an immense, rippling, bed of mineral turbulence. You can smell the danger in the air!

'Pilgrims come from everywhere and quickly become obsessed. I think of Shelley, of Raimondo di Sangro and his strange experiments, of the Order of the Golden Dawn ... My friends, look no further for your decadent city, your Eldorado, your Shangri-La! Tomorrow morning, if you agree, I shall set you on the path of discovery.'

While thanking Virgilio for his generous welcome, I could not help wondering why the bookshop had become a target for Catholic fanatics. Nothing causes me greater concern than to be told not to concern myself about something.

—=◦◯◦=—

After several days of total indolence, we began, under Virgilio's guidance, our tour of the Neapolitan underbelly. We soon found ourselves among old friends: priests of Isis, Hermes Trismegistus, Mithras, cults of the dead, miracle-working saints, necromancers, alchemists, rosicrucians, freemasons, poets, revolutionaries, psychics, theosophists, aesthetes, perverts of every age and provenance. Naples has been a magnet to so many! Even dear Leopardi, the poet who was to define for us with such surgical precision the true meaning of Decadent gardening – 'every garden is a hospital' – there he is, buried opposite the author of the Aeneid at the entrance to a Roman tunnel – once the site of orgies, now the path of a four lane highway.

One of our favourite places was the Cappella di Sansevero, right at the heart of the city, with its remarkable veiled Christ and sinister, alchemical crypt. This is the burial place of Raimondo di Sangro, Duke of Torremaggiore, Prince of Castelfranco and

Sansevero, scientist, publisher and magician, sometimes known as the Faust of Naples. He made a pact with the devil, so legend has it, in exchange for the innermost secrets of nature. As a student of law and philosophy at the Clementine College of Rome, he showed a particular interest in pyrotechnics. At the age of sixteen, in 1726, he inherited his princely titles and fortune – so often the prelude to a great Decadent career! The ground-floor windows of his palazzo in Vico Sansevero were observed to flash red, green and blue with his late-night experiments; hammers were heard smashing into anvils; there were muffled explosions and cries; and sometimes the ground shook as if to the rumbling of huge invisible wagons . . .

A keen alchemist, with a special fascination with the elixir of life, he executed two of his servants for trifling offences, mummified them with salts and trismegistical compounds, and opened them up so that their organs and blood vessels could be inspected. These two martyrs to alchemy are still on view in the vaults beneath the chapel, and we took to eating our sandwiches there at lunchtime to ponder on the mysteries of existence.

Raimondo tried many more experiments – he worked unsuccessfully on a perpetual light, artificial wax, and the desalination of sea-water – but his most ambitious project was for his own resurrection. As he felt his end approaching, he instructed a Moorish servant to cut him into pieces and place him in a special trunk – from which, after a process of re-integration – he would rise up as fit as a fiddle. Everything went perfectly until a member of his family, who was unaware of the experiment, opened the box before the appointed time. The Prince was only partially re-assembled. He started like a man woken suddenly from a deep sleep, tried to sit up, and fell back 'with the terrible cry of a soul in damnation'.

It is a feeling we know too well.

———=◦◉◦=———

We had been in Naples for a little less than a fortnight and everything about the city seduced us with its siren song of debauchery. One morning we received an invitation from our host to a rather amusing little gathering taking place that night in Pompeii. 'Petronius would have approved' was how he described it. He told us to wear something special.

We went out shopping at once among the troglodytic labyrinths of Spaccanapoli and found a pair of crimson leather togas that made us look magnificently louche. After a light supper of smoked eel and fresh marigolds, we slipped on a pair of trousers, some yellow crocodile shoes and raincoats, then took the Circumvesuviana railway to Pompeii.

Around us now, as we waited outside the kiosk, a silvery townscape glittered in the dark – every shop a sparkling cabinet of Ancient World kitsch: bare-breasted Venuses, statues of Cicero and Augustus, oil lamps and jugs in the form of grinning bacchic imbeciles. These drew from Durian one of his more fulsome panegyrics. In his opinion such objects demonstrate the yearning of ordinary, simple people for extravagance and grandeur – a leap onto a higher aesthetic plane which they are incapable of achieving on their own, weighed down as they are by their own stupidity and the crassness of popular taste. They have to be helped and guided by finer spirits. The fact that they long to fill their homes with pagan totems was proof of his great theory of life.

'Which is?' I asked.

'That inside every suburban man there's a Caligula waiting to burst out. And I feel more and more persuaded that this is our rôle, Medlar – to 'caligulize' the man in the street.'

The enormity of this truth suddenly impressed itself upon me with all the force of a lustful Catholic priest. It was a truly noble aim, and one which we are uniquely qualified to pursue. I felt that we should be proclaiming it from the rooftops. At the same time I thought that Durian was perhaps overlooking an important aspect. His concern for the man in the street was all very laudable, but what about the woman in the street? Had he thought of her?

'Of course. We must liberate her too, penetrate the dark prison of her inhibition, seek out the hidden Messalina, the whore of Dionysus, unshackle and electrify the terminals of her lust . . .'

This fascinating conversation is cut short by an incongruous figure stepping out of the shadows, his hair oiled and perfumed, his eyes ringed with kohl like a Fayyum portrait. He too wears a raincoat.

'Ah, Virgilio!'

We embrace. He bids us follow.

We pass tourist stalls and bars, shuttered and silent. Cats stalk amorously between the trees. We reach the gates of the ancient city.

Virgilio produces a key, and with a delicious sense of transgression we pass through the turnstiles, then up the deserted avenue towards the amphitheatre. Strange shapes of ancient masonry, silhouettes of temple and gymnasium, brothel and bath-house, loom against a pearly sky.

At the entrance to an imposing house, we stop. A gentle knock, and the door opens.

Inside, lamps are burning. Flame-lit faces and glimpses of frescoed wall – scenes of antique copulation, a man weighing an outsize penis on a set of scales. There is something Japanese in their graphic ingenuity: athletic angles are chosen to show these genital encounters, frozen in a Keatsian trance of 'winning near the goal'. The colours are bright, lurid, fresh.

We are discreetly parted from Virgilio, our coats are taken, and a young centaur with red-daubed cheekbones and ivy in his hair leads us to a private room.

Here, on a couch flanked by tall golden flambeaux, reclines a heavy-paunched man in his fifties. He wears the purple toga of the patrician. After scrutinising our attire approvingly he welcomes us with lugubrious formality.

'Members or guests?' he asks.

'Guests. With beautiful members.'

He permits himself a faint smile, then asks: 'What brings you here?'

'The secrecy, the scent of scandal, Virgilio's recommendation . . .'

'Do you have names?'

'We do.'

We briefly tell our story. Our host nods gravely, and rings a small china bell.

A man dressed as Hermes – naked, that is, but for hat and winged shoes, painted with magic symbols – enters the room and beckons us to follow. He leads us down to the courtyard, where Virgilio is waiting.

'Everything in order?'

'It would appear to be. The togas obviously delighted him.'

'Of course . . . Take a drink from the table and come into the garden.'

Our host has followed us and is keen to know more of the Decadent Restaurant. We describe it as best we can – its décors, its food, its air of theatrical illusion.

'Everything forbidden was permitted,' says Durian. 'And everything permitted was forbidden.'

'How refreshing,' says our host. 'I'm sorry I missed it. You really must recreate the place.'

'Ah, if only . . .' Durian waves a languorous hand, as if to follow our painted dream as it vanishes like smoke into the air.

A Frenchman named Maurice, a wild-looking fellow with Medusa hair, suddenly speaks up most energetically.

'It's not impossible, you know. Not at all.'

I take a good look at him. His wiry coiffure really is remarkable – it shoots out in all directions, held under control – I speak purely visually here – by a pair of arc-welding eyes and a goatee beard of immense precision rooted in a well-formed jaw.

'All you need is a few immensely rich backers,' he continues, 'the finest designers, and a couple of the best chefs in the world. I could fix it up for you. We can open in London or New York, prix fixe, paid in advance, no questions asked. We won't make any money of course . . .'

'And the police will come and close us down just as they did in Edinburgh,' says Durian.

Maurice laughs. 'But of course. That's part of the deal! People will flock to the place in the hope of seeing you arrested. Live policemen in action, marksmen, loudhailers, lights . . . *Un coup de théâtre!*'

'Having been through it once, I would describe it as more of a tragedy. There's nothing remotely amusing or aesthetic in being arrested.'

'Then do it as a show. You don't even need to be there. Use actors.'

Our host intervenes. 'If you need investors . . .'

'No,' I say. 'We're immensely touched, but it's too soon. Perhaps in a year or two, when our wounds have healed. But for now our pain is still too acute. The smell of betrayal and destruction is too strong in our nostrils; the memory, in a word, is too green.'

I wipe a small tear from my eye with my napkin, and for a moment the dark presence of the volcano above us takes possession of our hearts.

—⇒०◒०⇐—

Finally I came to understand why it is that certain more pious members of the local catholic community might be upset with Virgilio and his friends. Durian and I were just eating a hearty breakfast of toast and white truffles when Virgilio joined us and in a very conspiratorial tone asked us if we might be interested in taking part in a very ancient unique ritual which very few knew about and which would require us to swear an oath of secrecy. Furthermore, if we agreed to this he, Virigilio, could take no responsibility for the outcome. We did not need any persuasion.

That evening we drove in Virgilio's ancient Alfa to the small town of Isernia, one of the most ancient cities of the kingdom of Naples, situated in the province called Molise. We parked the Alfa in the town square and made our way toward the cathedral. Virgilio held out a small amulet to an emaciated, sinister-looking peasant standing guard at the door. The peasant nodded and we went in. Perhaps it was the contrast with the deserted square, but the moment I walked into the basilica I sensed an air of feverish expectation. There was a low hum emanating from the congregation which presaged something other than the customary litany of the year.

The three of us walked up the dimly-lit nave of the basilica and found seats towards the front. Virgilio greeted and shook hands with several of those who surrounded us. As my eyes became accustomed to the poor light I noticed the statue of a saint standing in front of the high altar. I asked Virgilio in a whisper who it was.

'St Cosimo,' he replied.

'It may be just a trick of the light, but from here it looks as if Saint Cosimo is sporting a large and powerful erection.'

'You're right, my friend. He is. But it is referred to as his 'big toe'.'

After a short bidding prayer, the priest sprinkled the saint with holy water and the statue was borne out of the basilica on the shoulders of six burly men. As it passed us, I was given the opportunity to see at close quarters just what a well-endowed young man Cosimo was. I also noticed the mixture of awe and veneration with which the saint's passing was greeted.

The congregation followed behind in a silent winding line. After fifteen minutes, we reached rising ground between two rivers about a mile from the town. On the most elevated part of this stood a church. Here the congregation re-assembled. As we were waiting to go in I noticed that many of the women were carrying wax amulets. Most of these comprised a ring below which hung a scrotum and penis viewed from the front. To the right a penis in profile and to the left a hand with the thumb poking out between the index and middle finger. Others included a sort of flying penis with wings and a chain between them. At the door they presented the amulets as ex-votos to a priest accompanied by the words *'San Cosimo benedetto, così lo voglio'* or *'San Cosimo, a te mi raccommando'*. The votive offering is presented with a gift of money and a kiss. *'Più ci metti, più meriti,'* mumbled a gnarled old woman – the more you put in, the more you deserve.

During the course of the mass, just before communion to be precise, half a dozen young men approached the altar rails, knelt down and spent some time deep in prayer. One of them I recognised from the bookshop. They then stood and turned to face the congregation. Each exposed their virile member to the public gaze and each wore an expression of profound piety. Many of the congregation, mostly women, pressed forward to make a closer examination. The priest, followed by an acolyte with a candle, picked up a small silver dish from the altar and came forward to stand in front of the first of the men. He effectively hid any view we had of the proceedings, but Virgilio explained that each one was suffering from impotence or some sort of penile dysfunction. Their virile members were being rubbed with St Cosimo's oil which was prepared according to the Roman ritual but with prayers said to the martyred saints Cosimo and Damiano. I heard the canon mutter the words *'Per intercessionem beati Cosmi, liberet te ab omni malo. Amen.'* Then he stepped back. We all pressed forward to see what change may have been effected. To general disappointment, the young man's prick hung glistening but limp, a disconsolate sight. Numbers four and six were the only ones which displayed any signs of tumescence. A very elegantly dressed woman in front of me was beginning to become quite agitated by the sight of this thickening and lengthening. Discussion was beginning to break out in small groups around the church. I assumed it was centred on the length of time any erections might be sustained. Attention was so riveted on these two we only slowly became aware of the state of the young man who had been the first to receive the blessed martyr's unction. His hands were still clasped devoutly in front of him, but his prick was now engorged and almost upright. His body was giving off small shudders. The congregation's rapt excitement was palpable. The young man's shudders increased in vehemence and regularity, until suddenly a long thick stream of semen erupted from his penis and splashed onto the stone floor of the church. Even before the second spurt appeared, pandemonium had broken out. Cries of *'miracolo'* filled the church and a number of women rushed forward to catch some of the ejaculate. I saw the elegantly dressed woman squatting down with her skirt pulled up around her waist. She was dipping her fingers in the pool of sperm and pushing them deep between her legs. Meanwhile the devout young man, who was still in the grip of a violent orgasm, was whisked away by two priests in the direction of the sacristy. A near hysterical crowd followed after. Those who failed to gain entry to the sacristy began hammering on the door with their fists. The rest were more interested in young men four and six. They were having more of St Cosimo's oil applied to their members by several young women in a most lubricious manner. One couple, obviously overcome by the entire occasion, had begun copulating on the steps of the altar. Where they led, others followed.

'When in Naples . . .' Virgilio smiled at us, taking his friend Salvatore by the hand.

The three others were still standing in front of the railings looking crestfallen, reduced to contemplating the reasons why the blessed martyrs might have forsaken them. Durian and I felt it incumbent upon us to take these young men in hand and see if we could not effect some less spiritual solution to their problems.

This was the beginning of a long and confusing night. My memory of it, I am afraid, is greatly obfuscated by narcotics and discretion . . .


The next moment I remember with any clarity was being awoken the following morning (or it may have been the morning after) by a loud shriek very close to my left ear. I knew it immediately to be Durian's, made recognisable by long acquaintance. He was naked, sitting bolt upright, looking down at the flaccid, but not unimpressive member which lay between his thighs.

'How did that get there?' he gasped in a voice tinged with horror.

'I think you've always had it,' I remarked, somewhat confused.

'Not that,' he retorted. 'That!'

On closer examination I noticed a somewhat shrivelled tattoo which had been applied to the shaft. It depicted in a delicate and intricate manner the great volcano which dominates the skyline behind Naples. It was some of the finest work of its kind I have come across. I did not know whether to express my envy or to laugh uproariously.

'Ah, so that was what that young Turkish boy was up to.'

'You mean you saw this happening. Why the hell didn't you stop him?'

'I saw you from a distance. You seemed to be enjoying yourself, judging by the stupid beatific grin on your face.'

'God, Medlar, what am I going to do? I'll have to have it removed.'

I was not certain of his meaning here, and advised caution.

'That sounds rather drastic. Why not enjoy it, old friend. Just think of the amusement it will cause when it erupts. I wonder if it'll register in the Richter scale, causing the death of thousands perhaps.'

Durian was not listening, or pretending not to listen.

'I look like some Hamburg rent boy!' he muttered petulantly.

'Yes. Some people get all the luck.'

It was only then that Durian looked about him and noticed, to his even greater horror, that we were in the open air, surrounded by an alarming quantity of countryside. To be more precise, we were lying under an olive tree on the slopes of Mount Vesuvius. An anonymous donor had thoughtfully provided us with blankets, a flask of coffee and some pressed figs for breakfast.

Durian seemed unable to enjoy the moment. He was undergoing a fit of anxiety, brought on partly by his new acquisition, partly by our exposure to a heavy dose of Nature. I, however, felt perfectly rested with a strange sense of superabundant calm, as if I had taken an elephantine dose of valerian.

'Can we be bothered to get up?' I offered languidly.

Durian did not seem to be listening.

'Perhaps we shall just have to wait here until we're rescued,' I said. 'Preferably by a shepherd boy.'

I wrapped the blanket around myself and rolled over.

Some time later I awoke again. Durian was looking a great deal better.

'The postman's been,' he said.

Next to the bowl of figs lay a heavy cream envelope with an embossed phallic crest on the flap. There was a card inside which told us that we were expected for lunch at the crater.

'I hope *The Crater* is the name of a restaurant, Medlar.'

'It's more likely to be the name of a crater,' I ventured.

'And where are we going to find one of those around here?' he asked.

I glanced for an instant at the slope where we lay. Below us Pompeii, Herculaneum, the Bay of Naples glittering in the sun.

Above, an appalling sight: a huge grey volcanic incline, running up to the sky.

'I expect we'll find one somewhere,' I said. 'We'll have a look after breakfast.'

Our intrepid expedition proved to be a simple matter of defying gravity. As we toiled along a dusty *via dolorosa* which snaked its way up the side of the volcano, Durian's temper got shorter and shorter in proportion to his breath. (Neither of us had taken so much exercise since we were underwent the assault course at the Kensington barracks of the Grenadier Guards. Mind you, we had not been informed exactly what sort of 'assault' this would entail). At length a passing bus driver took pity on our suffering. We were taken up into his bus and transported to the summit. Luckily nobody was around to witness the ignominy of our arrival.

At first the volcanic crater seemed barely worth the effort. For what seemed like an eternity we stood staring down into a vast blackened crucible of boulders and ash, offering nothing to the weary pilgrim but a thousand shades of grey. At that moment, the most profound feelings of despair, which I thought I had managed to slough off since our departure from Edinburgh, welled up once more in my breast and for an instant I believe Durian and I shared the same thought: that of casting ourselves hand in hand into the abyss, putting a fitting end to our miserable existence in this Vale of Tears. However, the scene also brought to mind a passage from de Sade's *Histoire de Juliette*, which I mentioned to my companion.

Juliette's encounter with her volcano begins thus:

*We dined at Pietra-Mala with the intention of going on to see the volcano. Ah, I can be so willingly seduced by all the irregularities of nature, loving everything which is characteristic of her disorders . . . her whims, and the heinous crimes she performs every day with her own fair hand! After a rather poor meal, despite the precaution we took of having a cook sent on ahead of us, we set off on foot across the arid, parched little plain where this natural phenomenon is to be seen. The surrounding landscape is sandy, stony and uncultivated. As we came closer we began to experience an excessive heat. We inhaled the smell of copper and charcoal given off by the volcano. Finally we noticed the flame from the crater which was made to burn even more fiercely by an unexpected shower of rain. This crater can be thirty or forty feet in circumference. If you plunge a tool into the earth round about, fire immediately bursts out under the impact. 'In the same way,' I said to Sbrigani who like me was contemplating this wonder, 'My imagination is fired by the thrust of a prick into my arsehole.'*

*The earth in the middle of the crater is baked black and consumed with fire. Round about, the earth is like potter's clay and gives off the same smell as the volcano. The heat from the crater is intense. Anything thrown into it is burnt up in an instant. It is violet in colour, like the flame of distilled wine. To the right of Pietra-Mala can be seen another volcano, which only erupts when a flame is applied to it. . . . When it has rained and the crater of this volcano has filled with water, this element comes boiling out and without losing any of its freshness. O nature, how whimsical you are!*

While Juliette, like Durian and I, stands contemplating the majesty of this natural wonder, other notions begin to inflame her mind.

*Other ideas, born out of the influence of climate on behaviour, presented themselves to me. When it occurred to me that in Sodom just as in Florence, and in Gomorra just as in Naples, and that around Etna as well as around Vesuvius, people were great devotees of and obsessed by buggery, I quickly came to the conclusion that the whimsical character of men resembles that of nature. Wherever nature herself is unbridled, she corrupts and depraves her children in turn. Thus I saw myself transported to those happy cities in Arabia. 'Here stood Sodom,' I said to myself. 'Let us pay homage to the morals of her inhabitants.' Thus I leant forward over the edge of the crater and presented my buttocks to Sbrigani, while watching Augustine do likewise with Zephir. Then we changed places. Sbrigani buried his prick deep into my maid's arse and I became the target of my valet's cock. While all this was going on, Augustine and I, face to face, frigged each other.*

Remembrance of this passage did something to lift our spirits.

Both Durian and I could feel ourselves pulling back from the abyss. Things livened up even more when our friends from last night began to appear one by one on the rim: the same lugubrious host, now in a rumpled suit and panama hat, Virgilio, as urbane as ever, and two of the young men who had the previous night received the blessed chrism of St Cosimo. Indeed one of them I recognised as the agent of the miraculous fountain. Cushions, umbrellas, plentiful wine and food were all that was required to transform this burnt-out chalice of rock into a place of companionship and luxury.

Conversation turned on the events in the church, how the Vatican might react when the news got out, whether they would need to protect themselves further from the fanatics of the Catholic right.

As the afternoon shadows lengthened, and the air of the gulf thickened into a luminous azure and ochre-tinted mist, Giovanni proposed a round of icy *limoncello* and a rendering of 'the old song'. He pulled a varnished mandolin from the depths of a picnic hamper, tuned its taut strings, and began to sing:

*Salve, sancte pater Priape rerum . . .*

Hail, Priapus, father of all.
Give me youth in flower,
Give me power, with shameless tool,
To please sweet girls and boys,
And chase away with games and toys
The cares that harm the soul.
Banish my fear of sad old age,
All thoughts of death and its pains,
Which drags us down to Avernus' shades
Where the dreaded tyrant reigns
And fate decrees an endless stay.
Hail Priapus, father, hail.
Come all onlookers and passers-by,
Nymphs who live in the sacred wood,
Nymphs who live in the sacred springs,
Come all, and with soothing voice
Sing songs to the comely lord:

'Hail, Priapus, father of all.'
Then cover his belly in kisses,
And garland with wreaths his tool,
Sing loudly in chorus again and again,
'Hail, Priapus, father of all.'
For he wards off the wicked and bloody,
He allows us to wander the woodland paths,
In peace and fearless ecstasy.
He keeps away vandals,
Whose crass feet slop through the sacred pools
And wash off their filth without tribute.
Sing to bold Priapus, Priapus the good,
'Hail, great father of all.'
Hail Priapus, potent friend,
Creator, progenitor of the world.
Or if you prefer, call him Nature, or Pan,
Since his brave vigour gave birth to all
In earth and sky and sea.
Jove himself at Priapus' call
Flings thunderbolts, and mad with love
Goes missing from his splendid halls.
Sweet Venus, hot Cupid, the Graces adore you,
And Bacchus the bringer of joy,
For without your power Venus is nothing,
The Graces graceless,
Bacchus a shadow, Cupid a dull boy.
Hail Priapus, potent friend.
Timorous virgins kneel in prayer,
And call you to loosen their long-tied belts.
The bride invokes you to bring her groom
With perfect potency and standing prick.
Hail, Priapus, father of all.

It was the perfect note on which to end the picnic.

—∘◉∘—

Virgilio's generosity as a host had been almost boundless. We had a room in his splendid house, with views across the bay, a fine table, exquisite wines, and an unfailing sense of welcome. We had cooked several strange meals for him – stuffed sow's womb, frogs in verjuice, calves' testicles with Karoly eclairs – to his endless delight. Like all Italians he had a keen sense of culinary propriety, and took almost indecent pleasure in seeing the rules broken.

In the normal run of things we would certainly have been tempted to overstay. But whether by design or accident, he started us on our way again with a casual remark.

'You should go round the corner some time and visit the house where Oscar Wilde lived.'

We did so, and gazed in a trance of incredulity at the huge white villa, its garden draped in bougainvillea and vines, its glittering Mercedes in the drive. I am deeply ashamed to admit it, but I had no idea that the divine Oscar had lived here. When we returned to Virgilio's house he had laid out the documentation: the Collected Letters, Ellmann's exquisite biography, a slim monograph by a local publisher, *Oscar Wilde a Napoli* . . . It was all there.

Oscar, we discovered, came to Naples in September 1897, three months after his release from Reading Gaol. 'I intend to winter here if all goes well. I love the place: it is, to me, full of Dorian and Ionian airs.' His plan was to live with his old amour, Bosie, because 'I cannot live without the atmosphere of Love: I must love and be loved, whatever price I pay for it . . . When people speak against me for going back to Bosie, tell them that he offered me love and that in my loneliness and disgrace I, after three months' struggle against a hideous Philistine world, turned naturally to him. Of course I shall often be unhappy, but still I love him: the mere fact that he wrecked my life makes me love him.'

After a short spell at the Hotel Royal des Etrangers they rented the Villa Giudice in Posillipo. Oscar posed as 'Sebastian Melmoth' – a suitably inconspicuous name, he thought, to disguise his identity. He worked on the final draft of *The Ballad of Reading Gaol*, made 'a few simple friends among the poorer classes' and learned to speak rather astonishing Italian. 'I believe I talk a mixture of Dante and the worst modern slang.' They visited Axel Munthe on Capri and Baron von Gloeden in Sicily – admiring his magnificent photographs of local boys posing naked among classical ruins. They went to the beach, the theatre, the cafés, living very much as Durian and I have lived on our travels, with a gaiety backed like a silvered mirror with a glittering layer of *tristesse*. For the Fates were sharpening their shears.

When Constance Wilde heard that her husband was living with Bosie, she wrote him a 'very violent letter': 'I *forbid* you to see Lord Alfred Douglas. I forbid you to return to your filthy, insane life. I forbid you to live at Naples.' To back up her veto she withdrew his allowance of £3 a week. (This, it appears, she had the right to do if he lived with a 'disreputable person'.) Oscar was bemused: 'I do not deny that Alfred Douglas is a gilded pillar of infamy,' he wrote, 'but I do deny that he can properly be described in a legal document as a disreputable person.' For some reason this defence did not work. The allowance was stopped.

Bosie's mother, Lady Queensberry, used similar blackmailing tactics. She nipped off her son's allowance of £25 a week and offered Wilde £200 if he would agree never to live in the same house with him again.

This pincer-movement was entirely effective. With no income, and too depressed to write, Oscar could not afford to be defiant. By the end of November he and Bosie had agreed to separate. Oscar wrote a long, bitter letter to his publisher, Leonard Smithers:

'*I wish you would start a Society for the Defence of Oppressed Personalities: at present there is a gross European concert headed by brutes and solicitors against us. It is really ridiculous that after my entire life has been wrecked by Society, people should still propose to exercise social tyranny over me, and try to force me to live in solitude – the one thing I can't stand. I lived in silence and solitude for two years in prison. I did not think that on my release my wife, my trustees, the guardians of my*

75

*children, my few friends, such as they are, and my myriad enemies would combine to force me by starvation to live in silence and solitude again. After all in prison we had food of some kind: it was revolting, and made as loathsome as possible on purpose, and quite inadequate to sustain life in health. Still, there was food of some kind. The scheme now is that I am to live in silence and solitude and have no food at all. Really, the want of imagination in people is appalling. The scheme is put forward on moral grounds! It is proposed to leave me to die of starvation, or to blow my brains out in a Naples urinal. I never came across anyone in whom the moral sense was dominant who was not heartless, cruel, vindictive, log-stupid, and entirely lacking in the smallest sense of humanity. Moral people, as they are termed, are simple beasts. I would sooner have fifty unnatural vices than one unnatural virtue. It is unnatural virtue that makes the world, for those who suffer, such a premature Hell.'*

There is defiance here, and Oscar's old, magnificent, hypocrite-withering fire, but this is practically the last time we find it in the letters. '. . . ruined, unhappy, lonely and disgraced. All pity, or the sense of its beauty, seems to me dead in the world.' 'What is there in my life for which I am not sorry? And how useless it all is! My life cannot be patched up. There is a doom on it.' He decided to move to Paris: 'It is my only chance of working. I miss an intellectual atmosphere, and am tired of Greek bronzes.'

Poor Oscar! As I read these letters, I felt like crying out to warn him that when a man is tired of Greek bronzes he is tired of life.

The most painful thing to bear was the feeling that he had been betrayed by Bosie. He wrote to Robert Ross in early March 1898:

*'The facts of Naples are very bald and brief. Bosie, for four months, by endless letters, offered me a 'home.' He offered me love, affection, and care, and promised that I should never want for anything. After four months I accepted his offer, but when we met at Aix on our way to Naples I found that he had no money, no plans, and had forgotten all his promises. His one idea was that I should raise money for us both. I did so, to the extent of £120. On this Bosie lived, quite happy. When it came to his having, of course, to repay his own share, he became terrible,*

*unkind, mean, and penurious, except where his own pleasures were*
*concerned, and when my allowance ceased, he left.*

*'With regard to the £500, which he said was a 'a debt of honour' etc.*
*he has written to me to say that he admits that is a debt of honour, but*
*that 'lots of gentlemen don't pay their debts of honour,' that it is 'quite a*
*common thing,' and that no one thinks anything the worse of them.*

*'I don't know what you said to Constance, but the bald fact is that I*
*accepted the offer of a 'home,' and found that I was expected to provide*
*the money, and that when I could no longer do so, I was left to my own*
*devices.*

*'It is, of course, the most bitter experience of a bitter life; it is a blow*
*quite awful and paralysing, but it had to come, and I know it is better*
*that I should never see him again. I don't want to. He fills me with*
*horror.'*

Despite the success of *The Ballad of Reading Gaol*, he remained
desperately poor. His health began to decline. Frank Harris suggested he write another comedy. Oscar replied: 'My dear Frank, I
have lost the mainspring of life and art, *la joie de vivre;* it is dread-
ful. I have pleasures, and passions, but the joy of life is gone. I am
going under: the morgue yawns for me. I must go and look at my
zinc-bed there.'

And so he did . . .

As we absorbed those terrible words, pressing on into the final
months of his humiliation and sickness, the whisky sank lower in
the bottle and a profound gloom came upon us. Oscar's fate
seemed our own. Exile, debt, loneliness. Sebastian Melmoth at
the door . . .

In the prime of youth and arrogance, or with money in the
bank, one can face such things easily. One can welcome Mr Melmoth, sit him down for a drink, listen to his appalling tale and
take in his sorrow without flinching. But we were not feeling
strong. By now Durian was sitting in an armchair with tears
streaming down his cheeks. The magic of Naples had evapor-
ated. Kind and generous as Virgilio was, we knew we had to
leave.

But *where* to go? This is the eternal question faced by the exile,
and therefore by the Decadent. It is, at times, unfathomable.

The world, we are told, is a solid sphere, with a definite girth, bulk, and other Euclidean properties. This may be true in some narrow scientific sense, but it bears no relation to the world as we see it, which is entirely elastic. Baudelaire begins his poem *Le Voyage*, with these words:

> *Pour l'enfant, amoureux de cartes et d'estampes,*
> *L'univers est égal à son vaste appétit.*
> *Ah! que le monde est grand à la clarté des lampes!*
> *Aux yeux du souvenir que le monde est petit!*

How small it is too in the eyes of exile! It seems like a stifling village, full of curious, hostile eyes.

I began, at last, to understand Durian's wish to die in a plane crash.

———o◉o———

I slept fitfully. As soon as sunlight began to filter through the shutters I got up, still haunted by my dreams of winged men in homburg hats and fur-collared coats. These were 'melmoths', bloated creatures that buzzed with a melancholy drone as they flew. Occasionally one would crash, attempting a tight turn, and burst in a mess of black fluid. The sight turned my stomach. I was watching the death of poor Oscar endlessly repeated in slow motion . . . I stumbled from the bedroom to Virgilio's kitchen, ready for coffee and another day of lethal thoughts.

It was painfully early, barely 8 o'clock. Virgilio had already left the house. I sat down at the kitchen table and waited for the coffee machine to spurt. Then I noticed, propped against last night's whisky bottle, a note addressed to us.

'Dear Medlar and Durian. An unpleasant-looking (and very evil smelling) man came to the house at six this morning, asking for you. I told him you had gone away for a few days. He did not seem to believe me. Call me at the shop if you need help. V.'

So. Henderson's were in town. The bloodhound bailiffs had sniffed us out. It was time to move on.

CAIRO

All journeys are haunted journeys – ours are anyway – if not by one of our spirit-ancestors among the pleasure-hounds of the nineteenth century, it's by Henderson's Debt Collection Agency. We wander, in short, in a bubble of memory and fear.

We came to Cairo more than usually tormented. Oscar was still with us – bloated, dying, miserable – he came to North Africa too of course, for boys and hashish, in the golden days – I just couldn't get rid of him. The spectre of poverty lingers horribly. Almost as long as the spectre of debt. How long would it take for the indefatigable John to trace us? We seemed to see his ghastly congested frame round every corner.

It was Robert Irwin, author of *The Arabian Nightmare*, diner at the Decadent, and *fin connaisseur du Moyen-Orient*, who first planted the city in our minds. We were discussing places of exile – the Crimea, Tahiti, Elba, New Mexico – someone mentioned Chislehurst, that exquisite choice of Napoleon III. Robert shook his encyclopaedic head – 'Cairo,' he said, staring into a glass of krupnik, 'is the perfect place to disappear.' We made a mental note, little thinking his advice would be needed before the year was out.

We arrived by moth-eaten train from Alexandria, a shadow of the rolling saloon described by Théophile Gautier when he came for the opening of the Suez Canal:

*The carriages are built in England, and painted white, with the classes indicated in English and Arabic. The first-class carriages are equipped with large green leather armchairs. There is a double ceiling to insulate the interior from the sun's heat, which would otherwise roast you alive. A hole in the centre forms a kind of ventilation shaft for the distribution of cool air, and openings at the sides are designed to make full use of even the slightest breeze.*

Gautier's journey was enlivened by visits to the poorer parts of the train, which had a special character of their own:

*The second-class compartments are connected like those on Swiss railways, with one important difference: at the end is a closed room reserved for the women – a kind of harem. The third class carriages are crude farm wagons with roofs, stuffed with fellahin, negroes, barabras and common people of all ages and types, who provide most of the railway's income and are enormously grateful for this form of transport, despite its utter lack of comfort and space.*

Something of this third class squalor survives from 1869. The elegance has all gone.

In Cairo we made at once for Shepheard's hotel, famed alike for its luxury and corrupting air of sloth. Here General Gordon, Richard Burton, Henry Morton Stanley, Sir George Margelle and other Victorian *oiseaux de paradis* had perched before swooping to an appointment with destiny at Mecca, Khartoum, or Ujiji. It was indeed a fabled place, radiant with the light of former days – where else could we stay? – there could be no other. But when we reached it, we had a nasty shock. Nationalists had burned it down in 1952. We were half a century too late.

By the ruins of Shepheard's we sat down and smoked a very desolate cigarette . . . How idiotic we had been! How crass! Why had we not bothered to find out?

Or rather, why had Durian not bothered?

He asked me the same question.

I answered him curtly.

His reply was vicious – mine even worse.

It got ugly.

I blamed Durian, he blamed me, we stung each other hard and often, as only old friends can. We were hot, frustrated, savage-tempered. No feelings were spared. The glare and heat of the sun seemed to drive us on. It was suddenly my fault that our restaurant had folded, our money was all gone, our glittering prospects reduced to a heap of dust. I flung this cheap accusation back in Durian's face – with full justification. He flinched – it was a palpable hit – tears filmed his eyes. At least one of us was feeling that the situation had been partially retrieved. However, rather than engage in vulgar triumphalism, I decided to show magnanimity. I sketched out a plan. I explained that we were going to buy a guide book. At first Durian was deeply offended by this. He said he would rather buy his own sister for sex than purchase a guide book. I did not doubt it for one moment and he was forced to admit this was not a good comparison. However, I proposed a compromise.

We entered a second-hand English book shop in Al-Gohar Street and searched through the shelves until we found a 1923 Baedeker. Its faded red binding would look handsome on a café table or in the pocket of a cream silk jacket. Its pages had gone yellow – a most appealing yellow, like that of an old meerschaum pipe. Most of the information in it was useless. The hotels and restaurants had long vanished. The archaeological descriptions predated the discovery of Tutankhamun and were preposterously out of date. For practical purposes it was no good at all.

To travel decadently, however, is more important than to arrive – there can be no doubt about that. This is our guiding principle. And with a seriously out-of-date guide book one can travel confident in the knowledge that one has not the slightest idea of where one will end up nor what one will see when one gets there. We bought the book at once.

A taxi took us to the Taverne du Champ de Mars – a superior bar where you can be sure to find at least some customers who know what it is to dress in leather. Over beer, hookahs and knick-knacks, illumination was swift to come on painted wings. Durian spotted a beautiful young Japanese reading at a nearby table.

'I think I shall go over and allow him the privilege of doing us a good turn,' he murmured.

Our oriental Ganymede was compliant. A brief consultation, and the decision was made: we would stay where he stayed, at the Hôtel du Nil.

The name alone was delicious, suggesting both the lush fecundity of the river and the emptiness – the nullity – of the desert. Indeed, I began to wonder, are the words Nile and Nil intimately related – the one a cipher for the other? The River Zero, fertilising the desert . . .

But I digress. I was speaking of the hotel.

I forget the precise terms in which this jewel of Africa was described to us, but the key points were all there: located in the heart of the brothel district, it had a lift lined with violet satin, iron bedsteads, clattering pipework, the barest of floorboards, and nicotine-coloured walls. How could we resist? If one cannot be magnificent at least one can be disreputable. The important thing is never to be banal.

We were shown to a dark and dilapidated room, with cracked, stained walls. It smelt of antiquity, nocturnal emissions and decay. Immediately, the haunting began. Durian threw open the shutters and gave a sudden involuntary shudder.

'Alesteir has been here! I can feel it.'

'Oh! And I can feel Gustave,' I replied. 'Dimly, Durian, but unmistakably. There's someone with him, but I wouldn't swear it's Maxime.'

'Perhaps it's Kuchuk Hanem.'

'Does she smell of rose water and the desert?'

'I rather think she does.'

'Then it can be no other.'

An auspicious start. We felt we were among friends.

Cairo is alive with restless ghosts. Their silvery vapour seeps up from the City of the Dead. It blends with the odours of spices from the bazaar, the sweet fumes of hashish and frangipani around the flower-market, the wail of street-merchants, musical klaxons and muezzin's cries in the labyrinth around al-Azhar, curling through shutters and slatted blinds, deep into the fan-stirred shadows of scented rooms.

It was in this great putrefying city, in 1904, that Alesteir Crowley received his vision that he was to be High Master of the Order of Thoth, Shambala of Ptah, Abbot of Thelema, Knight Elect of the Sangrail, Beast 666 of the Apocalypse.

His first visit to Cairo had taken place the previous year. He arrived with his wife Rose, not long after their wedding. During their time here he had persuaded her to spend a night with him in the King's Chamber of the Great Pyramid – by no means the most bizarre of the conjugal duties she was expected to perform. Here he was hoping to invoke the figure of Thoth, the Egyptian god of wisdom with the head of an ibis. He wrote:

*We reached the King's chamber after dismissing the servants at the door of the Grand Gallery. By the light of a single candle placed on the edge of the coffer I began to read the invocation. But as I went on I noticed that I was no longer stooping to hold the page near the light. I was standing erect. Yet the manuscript was not less but more legible. Looking about me, I saw that the King's Chamber was glowing with a soft light which I immediately recognised as the astral light. . . . The King's Chamber was aglow with the brightest topical moonlight. The pitiful dirty yellow flame of the candle was like a blasphemy, and I put it out. The astral light remained during the whole of the invocation and for some time afterwards, though it lessened in intensity as we composed ourselves for sleep.*

When Crowley and Rose returned the following year he began preparing himself for an event which would prove to be the most significant of his life.

The first stage of this preparation entailed a change of name. The prosaic Mr and Mrs Alesteir Crowley vanish and are reincarnated as the Prince and Princess Choia Khan. He wears a robe of silk and coat of cloth of gold. His turban is enlivened with a spray of gems and he carries an Indian sword at his side. As he drives through the streets of Cairo in a carriage, a passage is cleared by two men running on ahead.

The royal couple take a flat in a building on the corner of a street near the Boulak Museum. (Needless to say when Durian and I went looking for it we discovered that the museum no longer existed). The Great Beast immediately sets about turning one of the rooms into a temple. While the white-robed Prince Choia Khan prostrates himself before the altar and utters interminable incantations, the Princess wanders around in a trancelike state. Her husband is convinced she is either drunk or suffering from hysteria brought on by her pregnancy. She keeps repeating the words: 'They are waiting for you,' and uttering the name of Horus, which is strange coming from someone who knows nothing of Egyptology. Furthermore, four days after they move in she mentions that Prince Choia Khan has offended 'the one who waits for Horus' and needs to beg forgiveness.

The couple visit a museum to see if it will provide some answers. They go up the stairs and find themselves in a long dimly-lit corridor. Princess Choia Khan stops and gestures towards a glass case at the far end. The gesture is accompanied by the words: 'There he is. There he is.' As they approach the case, Crowley begins to make out in the half-light an image of the Ibis-headed god, Horus, painted on a wooden funeral slab. This alone is enough to unsettle him. But something else leaves him awe-struck. The exhibit is designated by a number. And the number is none other than 666. The Number of the Beast! His number!

They hurry back to the temple and he continues the invocation with renewed vigour. A bowl of blood and a sword are now placed on the altar.

*'Come thou forth and dwell in me; so that every Spirit, whether of the Firmament, or of the Ether, or of the Earth or under the Earth; on dry land or in the Water, or Whirling Air or of Rushing Fire; and every spell and scourge of God the Vast One may be THOU.'*

The Prince is convinced that the Egyptian god will appear to him and that he is destined to lead Mankind into a New Aeon. Meanwhile the Princess Choia Khan undergoes another meta-morphosis. She becomes Ouarda the Seeress – Ouarda is the Arabic word for 'rose' – and maintains that 'the Equinox of the Gods has come'. This pronouncement is swiftly followed by the appearance of the Prince's Guardian Angel to Ouarda. She tells her husband that the Guardian Angel, Aiwass by name, wants him to enter his temple and write down everything he hears.

Consequently on April 8th 1904, on the stroke of midday, Prince Choia Khan enters his temple with a pen and sheaves of paper which he sets down on a desk. He sits, and waits.

Suddenly, behind him from the corner of the room , a voice emerges, 'solemn, voluptuous, tender, fierce . . .' It announces itself as 'Had! The manifestation of Nut.' Crowley hurriedly cop-ies down 66 verses of utterance. It takes an hour, at the end of which Aiwass the Guardian Angel disappears.

The next two days follow the same pattern and Aiwass com-pletes his communication. This will become known as the Great Revelation in Cairo and the book of prophecy it will give rise to is the *Liber Legis* or *Book of the Law*. There is little doubt that Crowley intended the work as an exercise of self-aggrandisement. *'Now ye shall know that the chosen priest and apostle of infinite space is the prince-priest the Beast.'*

Be that as it may, there are still many pronouncements which are dear to our hearts. Hence: *'To worship me take wine and strange drugs whereof I will tell my prophet and be drunk thereof,'* and *'There is no law beyond "Do what thou wilt."'* *'Be strong, O man! Lust, enjoy all things of sense and rapture: fear not that any God shall deny thee for this.'*

Aiwass certainly was no liberal humanist . . . *'Mercy be let off; damn them who pity! Kill and torture; spare not; be upon them!'* In fact it was only later that Crowley came to understand who Aiwass really was. During the course of the Angel's pronouncement, Crowley managed to sneak a look at him and, although suspended in the midst of a cloud, Crowley described him as *'a tall dark man in his thirties, well knit, and eyes veiled lest their gaze should destroy what they saw.'* And many years later he was to refer to him in *The Magical Record*: *'And her (the Scarlet Woman's) concoction shall be sweet in our mixed mouths, the Sacrament that giveth thanks to Aiwaz, our Lord God the Devil.'*

Thus in that small flat in Cairo, Crowley had caught a glimpse and copied down the words of Satan!

And perhaps we too would be vouchsafed a vision during our stay. Certainly Durian was thinking along these lines.

For the moment we contented ourselves with the pleasures of Cairo life, wandering through al-Jamaliyah, haggling in the Khan al-Khalili, sipping coffee at the fading azimuth of fiery afternoons. At a bath-house one evening, in the hands of a skilled masseur, Durian notched up his most prolonged and copious orgasm ever – it beat even the great Cricket Pavilion Orgasm of 1969 for intensity. (I was jealous until I bettered it with one of mine.)

Between visits to the masseur and the coffee-house, we spent hours reading. Like a clifftop hotel, Cairo offers tremendous views – backwards through time.

One of the great vanished sights – which we had to content ourselves with imagining – was the dervishes. They provided a kind of fanatical circus show for Victorian tourists. William

Holman Hunt and his friend Thomas Seddon watched them celebrate the Prophet's birthday:

*Finding the door of the sheikh's house open, we went in, and found a great many Europeans there, with a crowd of Arabs, kawasses, dervishes, and men and boys of all nations. Seats were ranged on each side for the Europeans. We came in at about eleven, and had to wait more than two hours before the sheikh arrived. During the interval, a number of jugglers and serpent-tamers performed their evolutions. Two men, very wildly dressed, went through some very bad sword-and-buckler exercise. Then men came in with pointed iron spikes, about fifteen inches long, with a large knob of iron at one end, garnished with short chains. These they stuck in the corners of their eyes, and twirled them round; then they dug the pointed end against their heads and bodies; then a man lay down, and they placed the pointed end on his stomach, whilst a man stood upon it; then they held four or five on the ground, point uppermost, and the jugglers walked on them; they then brought in skewers, and thrust them through their cheeks and arms, and through the flesh on their bodies, having stripped to the waist.*

*The performance began now to be very disgusting: they foamed at the mouth, and seemed to become intoxicated, falling back into the arms of those behind them, apparently fainting. One man howled, growled like a lion, and raved like a maniac. This continued for some time, when the serpent-men came in with the asps round their necks; and then some of the fanatics rushed on the snakes, and tore them with their teeth; and when four or five men held them each, they struggled fearfully, and tried to bite them.*

*As the banners now appeared, the lower order of them lay down side by side on their faces, while the others, better dressed, took them by the legs and shoulders, and pressed them closely together. By the time that a compact mass was formed, half-a-dozen turbaned dervishes, with long sticks, rushed in over them; and then the sheikh, on horseback, a man leading his frightened horse, who trod heavily and quickly, like a horse passing through a bog. He swerved, and trod on one man's head, and on the legs of others. The sheikh sat lying back, as if stupefied and in pain, dressed in a huge green turban, and supported by a dervish on each side. Some of the men were lifted up as if hurt, and all seemed to be, or to sham an intoxicated ecstasy.*

We were sorry to miss a show of this calibre. It had exactly the atmosphere we liked to create at the Decadent restaurant.

Another attraction – also now suppressed – was the slave market, visited by the painter William Müller in 1839:

*One enters this building, which is situated in a quarter the most dark, dirty, and obscure of any at Cairo, by a sort of lane; then one arrives at some large gates. The market is held in an open court, surrounded with arches of the roman character. In the centre of this court the slaves are exposed for sale, and in general to the number of from thirty to forty, nearly all young, many quite infants. The scene is of a revolting nature; yet I did not see, as I expected, the dejection and sorrow I was led to imagine. The more beautiful of the females I found were confined in a chamber over the court. They are in general Abyssinians and Circassians. When any one desires to purchase, I not unfrequently saw the master remove the entire covering of the female – a thick woollen cloth – and expose her to the gaze of the bystander. Many of these girls are exceedingly beautiful – small features, well formed, with an eye that bespeaks the warmth of passion they possess. The negresses, on the contrary, have little to please; they disgust, for their hair is loaded with two or three pounds of a sort of tallow fat, literally in thick masses, and as this is influenced by the heat of the sun, it gradually melts over the body, and the smell from it is disagreeable in the extreme; yet in this place did I feel more delight than in any other part of Cairo: the groups and the extraordinary costume can but please the artist. You meet in this place all nations. When I was sketching – which I did on many occasions – the masters of the slaves could in no manner understand my occupation, but were continually giving the servant the price of the different slaves, to desire me to write the same down, thinking I was about to become a large buyer.*

Cairo in those days was a place of magic, charlatans and bizarrely sordid spectacle. Little of this remains – and yet we loved it. It was here, after all, that Gustave Flaubert and his friend Maxime du Camp boarded their boat for a four-month trip up the Nile in February 1850 – one of the great decadent journeys of history. They started, as luck would have it, from the Hôtel du

Nil. We could not ignore them. They called to us. It was time now to pay them homage.

Gustave and Maxime were dutiful tourists. They rode out to the pyramids, smoked a pipe in front of the sphinx ('it watches us with a terrifying gaze'), visited mosques, bazaars, cemeteries and Turkish baths. They called on consuls and Coptic theologians, went hunting, watched a wedding and a ritual trampling, sampled the Cairo brothels.

In his diary, Gustave describes an evening 'chez la Triestine'. He notes the shaved pubis of Hadély, her 'bronze buttocks' and hard, cool flesh – and her bed full of cats. Despite the exotic surroundings it is not a particularly pleasurable encounter – 'dry and fatty . . . The total effect is one of plague and leprosy'. Later, she helps him dress and asks questions in Arabic. His servant Joseph, who has been present throughout, translates the conversation. How strange, remarks Gustave, to make love through an interpreter!

They also visit a couple of hospitals.

*23 December. Caserlaïneh. Well maintained . . . pretty cases of the pox. In the Mamelukes' ward several have it in their arses – at a sign from a doctor they all stood up on their beds, untied their belts (it was like a military manoeuvre) and opened their anuses with their fingers to show their chancres. Enormous infundibula – one had a wad of gauze up his arse. Totally skinless prick on one old man – I had to step back at the smell that came off it. . . .*

*26 December. Civil hospital, Ezbekkiya. Madmen yelling in their cells – an old man weeping and begging to have his throat cut. A man claiming to be 'the great princess's black eunuch' came and kissed my hand. An old woman invited me to make love, showed me her long skinny breasts dangling and flapping around her navel. She leaned her head to one side and showed me her teeth, her smiles exquisitely sweet. Seeing me in the courtyard, she stood on her head and displayed her bottom – her custom whenever a man appears. A woman danced in her cell, playing her metal chamber pot like a drum.*

On February 5, they spent their first night in the boat –

'devoured by fleas by way of inauguration'. The following afternoon they set sail for Upper Egypt. The weather was fine; the sailors sang and danced.

One purpose of the trip was to take photographs of Egyptian temples. Photography was only recently invented and had barely been seen in Egypt before. Du Camp brought along all the bulky apparatus required, and had it carried by members of the crew. To provide a 'uniform scale of proportions' for his pictures, he sent one of the sailors, a muscular young Nubian called Hadji Ismael, to stand by the monument. It was hard to make the fellow stand still, and Maxime had to resort to a trick, telling him that the brass tube at the front of the camera was a cannon, which would shoot him dead if he moved. This 'immobilized him totally,' Du Camp recorded, 'as you may see from my plates.'

At Dendera, he overheard a touching conversation between Hadji Ismael and Rais Ibrahim, the captain of their boat:

– Well, Hadji Ismael, what news?
– Nothing special. The father of thinness [Du Camp] told me to climb a column bearing the giant face of a god. He wrapped the black veil around his head. Then he pointed his golden cannon and shouted, 'Keep still!' The cannon watched me with its bright eye but I did not move at all, and it did not kill me.
– Allah is great, said Rais Ibrahim.
– And Lord Mohammed is his Prophet.

On March 6, they reached Esneh, a town of exiled courtesans – the ruler of Egypt was strictly Boys' Own and wouldn't have female dancers or prostitutes in the capital. Among the inhabitants of Esneh was the celebrated Kuchuk Hanem. Gustave's night with her is one of the finest, most complete episodes in the history of Decadence.

We enter the small courtyard of a house. On the stairs, facing us, a woman waits – she is surrounded by light and stands out against the blue sky. She wears pink trousers, and is bare above the waist but for a deep violet veil.

She has just come from the bath – her firm breasts smell fresh, with a *scent like sugared turpentine. She perfumes our hands with rose water.*

*We go in on the first floor, turning left at the top of the stairs into a square, whitewashed room: two divans – two windows – one looks onto the mountains, the other onto the town.*

*Kuchuk Hanem is a big, splendid creature – whiter than an Arab – she is from Damascus. Her skin is slightly coffee-coloured. When she sits you see little folds of bronze along her sides. Her eyes are black and immense, her eyebrows dark – nostrils flared – broad, solid shoulders, full breasts like apples. She wears a wide tarboosh, crowned with a convex golden disc, a green emerald-like stone at its centre. The blue tassle of the tarboosh spreads like a fan, caressing her shoulders. Along its front edge, a little spray of artificial flowers is fixed to her hair, which is black, curly, rebellious to the brush – her tresses are parted, and join at the nape of her neck. One of her teeth, an upper right incisor, is starting to rot.*

*Her bracelet is a pair of twisted golden rods. Triple necklace of large hollow golden grains. Her earrings are golden discs, slightly bulbous, with little specks of gold around the rim. Tattooed on her right arm is a line of blue writing.*

*She asks if we wish to be entertained. Maxime says he would like to be entertained first, on his own – they go into a room on the ground floor. After M. Ducamp it's M. Flaubert's turn.*

*The musicians arrive: a child and an old man with a rag over his left eye. They both scrape the rebabeh, a small round violin ending in an iron spike. It has two horsehair strings and a disproportionately long neck. No sound could be more tuneless or disagreeable. The musicians play on and on; we have to shout to make them stop.*

*Kuchuk's dance is as brutal as a kick in the backside. She squeezes her bosom in her jacket so that her two bare breasts are pressed together – when she dances she wraps a gold-striped brown shawl like a belt around her, with three tassles hanging on ribbons. She lifts herself now on one foot now on the other, a remarkable sight: one foot on the ground, the other rising and crossing her calf, all with a light springing step. I have seen this dance on ancient Greek vases.*

*Bambeh, her servant, likes to dance in a straight line – she lowers and raises just one haunch – a kind of rhythmic limping of great character. Bambeh has henna on her hands (she worked as a chamber-maid for an*

*Italian household in Cairo – she understands a few words of Italian – has a slightly diseased eye.) Otherwise their dancing – apart from Kuchuk's special step – is hardly to be compared with Hassan el Bilbesi [a male dancer in Cairo]. Joseph thinks all beautiful women dance badly.*

*Kuchuk picks up a drum – superb pose as she plays it – drum on her left thigh, left elbow lowered, wrist raised, fingers slightly splayed as they strike – right hand keeping the beat – head thrown splendidly back, torso arched.*

*These women and the old musician take in considerable amounts of raki.*

*Kuchuk dances with my tarboosh on her head. She leads us to the back of her room and mounts each of us in turn, strutting and cracking jokes like a good catholic tart.*

*We take coffee in a palm-leaf shack with sunlight dappling the mats where we sit. Kuchuk's delight at our shaven heads and Max saying 'La illah Allah Mohammed rassoun Allah'.*


*Second, more detailed visit to the temple. Dinner.*


*We return to Kuchuk's house. The room is lit by three oil lamps on tin girandoles fastened to the wall. The musicians are in their places. Drinks are taken swiftly. Our gifts and sabres have their effect.*

*In comes Saphiah-Zougairah – small woman with a large nose and deep-set black eyes, lively, fierce and sensual. Her necklace of piastres rattles like a pony-trap. She comes in and kisses our hands.*

*The four women sit in a row on the divan and sing. The lamps form trembling rhomboids of yellow light on the walls. Bambeh wears a pink dress with wide, pale sleeves, her hair covered with a black scarf, fellah-style. Everyone sings, the drums thud, the monotone rebecks provide a soft, insistent bass.*

*I go downstairs with Saphiah Zougairah – wicked as hell, constantly on the move, loves it – a little tigress. I stain the divan.*

*Second time with Kuchuk. As I kiss her shoulder I take the beads of her necklace between my teeth. Her velvety quim with its soft folds. I feel filthy. Ferocious.*

*Kuchuk dances The Bee for us. First we send out Fergalli and another sailor – they have watched the previous dances and provided the grotesque element in the scene; then we blindfold the child with a black veil, and the old musician with a length of his blue turban. Kuchuk strips as she dances. When she's naked, she keeps just a handkerchief, pretends to hide behind it, then throws it aside – that's the bee.*

*She dances only briefly; she doesn't enjoy The Bee much any more. Joseph is red-faced and very excited. He claps his hands: 'La, en, nia, oh! En, nia, oh!' At the end, after hopping with that famous step, legs passing across each other, she comes panting back to the couch and lies down, her body still pulsing to the beat. She picks up a pair of large rose-striped trousers – climbs into them up to her neck – the musicians are unveiled.*

*She crouches – magnificent, completely sculptural design of her knees.*

*Another dance: a cup of coffee is placed on the floor, she gyrates in front of it, then drops to her knees and continues to sway the upper half of her body, still playing her finger-cymbals and making a kind of swimming stroke with her arms. Her head gradually sinks till she reaches the rim of the cup – then grips it in her teeth and leaps up with a sudden bound.*

*She is worried about us spending the night with her – there are robbers who come when there are foreigners about. She shows us a couple of bodyguards – 'ruffiano, buono ruffiano', she says – slapping them and kicking their backsides for a joke. The guards bed down in a ground floor room between the voluptuary chamber and the kitchen.*

*In the evening, as the dancing goes on, I take a short stroll in the street – one very bright star shines in the northwest, over a house to my left. Utter silence. Only Kuchuk's window lighted. The sounds of music and the women's voices singing.*

*Her servant, who spends the night in the next room with Joseph and the guards, is an Abyssinian slave, a negress with a round plague scar on each arm – like a burn or blister, but less regular in shape. Her name is Zeyneb. When Kuchuk calls her in the night she drags on the first syllable: 'La, Ze-eyneb – la, Ze-eyneb'.*

*We lie down. She wants the outside of the bed. The lamp is a wick resting in an oval bowl. Her body is sweaty from dancing – she feels cold. After a violent gamahuche, a second 'coup'.*

*She sleeps with her hand in mine, fingers entwined. She snores. The feeble light of the lamp makes a pale metallic triangle on her lovely* forehead – the rest of her face in shadow. Her little dog sleeps on my silk jacket on the bed.

She complains of a cough, so I lay my pelisse over her blanket.

I hear Joseph and the guards chatting in low voices in the next room. I think of other nights when I have watched women sleeping – and all the nights I have spent awake. I think about everything, I rack myself with sadness and dreams, and pass the time by crushing fleas on the wall, making long red and black arabesques on its white surface.

I feel her stomach on my buttocks; her motte – warmer than her belly – heating me like an iron. Another time I doze off with my finger hooked under her necklace, as if to hold onto her when she wakes up.

I think of Judith and Holophernes. How flattering it would be to leave a memory behind when we go – will she think of us more than others, keep us in her heart?

At 2.45 she wakes – another 'coup', full of tenderness. We hold hands, really loving each other – or so I choose to believe. Even as she sleeps she squeezes my hands and presses me with her thighs in a rhythmic, almost mechanical way, like an unconscious shudder of pleasure. I smoke a chicheh, and she goes off to chat with Joseph. I wander out into the street – stars shining, the heavens very high. Kuchuk returns with a pot of glowing coals – she warms herself for an hour, huddled over it, then comes back to bed. The pot of coals is at the head of the bed. She sleeps, her blanket pulled over her head. 'Basta.'

In the morning we calmly say farewell. Our two sailors carry the luggage to the boat. We go off hunting around Esneh – cotton fields under the palms and gazi trees – Arabs, donkeys, buffalo on their way to the fields – the wind whistling through the thin branches of the gazis as it does through the reeds at home. The sun rises – the mountains change colour, no longer the tender pink we saw as we left Kuchuk Hanem's.

The fresh air feels good on my eyes. Hadji-Ismael, my escort, leans forward from time to time, to show me doves hidden among the branches. I barely see them . . .

I keep thinking this morning of the Marquis de Pomereu's ball at le Héron, when I walked all alone in the park, after the dance. It was during the school holidays, between my third and fourth years.

I return to the boat to fetch Joseph. We buy meat, a belt, ink from the mosque. The school is full of children writing on boards.

We meet Bambeh and the woman who played the drum. Bambeh buys *our bread for us – she looks exhausted. We leave Esneh at a quarter to twelve . . .*

This account comes from Flaubert's intimate journal. When he showed it, a few years later, to his lover Louise Colet, she was appalled by the squalor of the scene. She was also rather jealous. Flaubert explained himself:

*As for Kuchuk Hanem, there is no need to worry. The orient is not as you imagine it. She felt nothing, I promise; even physically, I suspect. She thought us excellent seigneurs because we were generous with our money, but that is all . . . The oriental woman is essentially a machine: to her, one man is much the same as another. Smoking, bathing, eyelid-painting and drinking coffee – that is the circle of their lives. As for physical enjoyment, it must be minimal, since the famous button, the source of a woman's pleasure, is cut off at an early age . . .*

*You say that her fleas degrade her for you. That was precisely what attracted me. Their sickening smell mixed with the scent of her skin, streaming with sandalwood. I want a touch of bitterness in everything, a hoot of mockery in our moments of triumph, even desolation in our enthusiasm. It reminds me of Jaffa, where, as I entered the town, I caught in the same instant the scent of lemon trees and the stench of corpses; the smashed-up cemetery was full of rotting skeletons, while the green trees dangled their golden fruits above our heads. Do you not feel the completeness of this as poetry? It really is the great synthesis.*

Like Maxime and Gustave, we contemplated the Sphinx and the pyramids, lost in wonder at the extravagance of human effort that went into their construction. Truly, this was decadence in stone! (The nearest we had ever come to such a feat was creating a marzipan replica of this magnificent ensemble for a masonic dinner at the restaurant. That alone had been a labour of love for Toni, our pastry chef, requiring three days' work and thirty-five kilogrammes of almonds, as well as large quantities of stimulants. The poor man was a wreck at the end of it.) But think of building that monster in the desert! Full size! With such primitive technology . . . The mind languishes at the thought. Yet there must have been consolations – the energy, the satisfaction – and, of course, the sight of all those slaves straining under the lash. It must have been profoundly sordid and exciting.

The pyramids, as any Student of Esoterica will tell you, were built as giant space laboratories which were too heavy for the rocketry of the day and never managed to get off the ground. Or possibly as star chambers from which the bodies of dead kings could be revived by the light of Orion passing down angled shafts into their mummified orifices. Or were they, as some say, built by extraterrestrials – as military outposts of a doomed colonial mission? It barely matters. The connection with the stars is beyond doubt, and for many reasons – from their configuration on the ground (a replica of Orion's belt), to the sheer fact that so many deranged people believe in this theory that it is dangerous to contradict them.

Ever since, as schoolboys, Durian and I huddled together at Lucan Lodge on that distant July night in 1969, watching Buzz Aldrin and Neil Armstrong bounce like sedated trampolinists across the moon, I have nursed a deep longing to go into space: to don that puffy white regalia, to climb, waving like Liberace, into the tiny cockpit at the top of a Titan rocket – then to be flung in a torrent of fire towards the stars!

Alas, neither of us have the physique, never mind the mentality, for the job. NASA require their astronauts to be A1 specimens. As representatives of the F class ('totally unsuitable material, lacking in endurance, know-how and moral character') we were never likely to make the grade – although our names are held on file in Brussels as volunteers, should the Kingdom of Belgium ever wish to start a space programme. We remain at full readiness, awaiting the call.

In the meantime we content ourselves with imaginary journeys into space. We have tried various forms of 'virtual reality' (a concept, like 'virtual orgasm', which fails to deliver on several fronts). Films are a help, of course, as are flight simulators, and a certain amount of 'flying ointment' (i.e. henbane; see *The Decadent Gardener*, page 148).

By far the most effective method we have found is to sit in a darkened room with a small reading-lamp, a glass of plum brandy, and a copy of that classic of space literature, *Carrying the Fire*.

Its author is Michael Collins, a test pilot and astronaut with an unusual view of existence (due partly, no doubt, to a working life carried out at an average speed of 22,000 miles per hour). He was the man, in Apollo XI, who stayed in the command ship orbiting the moon while Aldrin and Armstrong flew down for a stroll among the boulders. Call him an observer, a voyeur, what you will – his lonely position gave him the leisure to contemplate the mysteries of their task. This was beyond his companions – they were too busy with the practicalities of fuel consumption, angle of descent, and not smashing into rocks. Collins was something of a poet – he put into words the sensations, thoughts and emotions of an earthling who is suddenly shot into space. His account is splendid. It earns him an honoured place in the Temple of Decadence.

His gifts first caught our attention when he described the cramped Gemini 10 spacecraft as 'an orbiting men's room'; and again when he spoke of the medical examinations at the School of Aerospace Medicine in Texas: 'no orifice is inviolate, no privacy respected'. (Suddenly, space travel took on exciting new possibilities in our minds.)

One of the finest moments in the book is an account of urinating in a space-suit. It is, apparently, something that everyone wants to ask an astronaut. He quotes the technical manual in full.

*Operating Procedure*
*Chemical Urine Volume Measuring System (CUVMS) Condom Receiver*

1. *Uncoil collection/mixing bag from around selector valve.*
2. *Place penis against receiver inlet check valve and roll latex receiver onto penis.*
3. *Rotate selector valve knob (clockwise) to the 'Urinate' position.*
4. *Urinate.*
5. *When urination is complete, turn selector valve knob to 'Sample.'*
6. *Roll off latex receiver and remove penis.*
7. *Obtain urine sample bag from stowage location.*

8. *Mark sample bag tag with required identification.*
9. *Place sample bag collar over selector valve sampler flange and turn collar 1/6 turn to stop position.*
10. *Knead collection/mixing bag to thoroughly mix urine and tracer chemical.*
11. *Rotate sample injector lever 90 degrees so that sample needle pierces sample bag rubber stopper.*
12. *Squeeze collection/mixing bag to transfer approximately 75 cc. of tracered urine into the sample bag.*
13. *Rotate the sample injector lever 90 degrees so as to retract the sample needle.*
14. *Remove filled urine sample bag from selector valve.*
15. *Stow filled urine sample bag.*
16. *Attach the CUVMS to the spacecraft overboard dump line by means of the quick disconnect.*
17. *Rotate selector valve knob to 'Blow-Down' position.*
18. *Operate spacecraft overboard dump system.*
19. *Disconnect CUVMS from spacecraft overboard dump line at the quick disconnect.*
20. *Wrap collection/mixing bag around selector valve and stow CUVMS.*

This is less a set of instructions than a prose poem! Step 4 (*'Urinate.'*) has the simplicity of a sketch by Ingres. One can almost feel the sense of relief as this brusque command cuts through the tangle of formalities that precede it . . . And instruction 19, I feel, has a similar cadence to some of the finer verses of Allen Ginsberg

But it is not only Cosmic Micturition that has long occupied my imagination. What of weightless copulation? Surely space travel would be worth it for this experience alone. The possibility is beautifully captured by our dear friend, the poet Neil Rollinson.

> *Fucking in zero gravity*
> *is something else,*
> *as Jan from the Particle Lab*
> *ably convinced me.*

*We clung to each other*
*like sky divers, amazed*
*at such demulcent air,*
*the absence of weight,*
*the acrobatic grace*
*of our bodies.*
*I'd like you to come*
*in my mouth, she said,*
*the pump of her fist moving us*
*smooth as a punt; and I came*
*unhindered by gravity,*
*in one straight line*
*like peas from a pea-shooter;*
*and Jan swam after them*
*sleek as a dolphin*
*taking the salty beads*
*in her mouth.*
*I imagined them travelling*
*to Alpha Centauri,*
*the pearls of my semen,*
*moving through space*
*like a notion*
*in Einstein's head,*
*and we laughed at that*
*for a long time*
*and lay in each other's arms,*
*spinning like satellites*
*over the lab.*

It was during these first few days in Cairo that I began to experience another form of travel which I would like to claim as the quintessential form for the Decadent.

I had been spending time out in the desert at night. I would be taken by taxi to an isolated spot and there walk a little way into the vastness before lying wrapped in a blanket contemplating the blue-black sky and the vast expanse of myriad stars above my head. They seemed as numberless as the grains of sand beneath me. Often a concerned taxi driver would find me in a state of near collapse and have to help me back to the vehicle. I would return to our hotel room in a state of emotional intensity, feverish perhaps, where exhaustion and elation combined to form a heady cocktail.

I was lying in bed one night in such a state drifting between sleep and wakefulness, when I sensed a light filling the space of the hotel window. At first I thought it was the coming of daylight but it appeared too swiftly and was too white in colour. A few moments after the appearance of the glow, my body began to shake horribly, although the shaking was so regular that it might better be described as 'vibrating'. I tried moving and calling out to Durian but was incapable of either. The vibrations began to build in intensity. My whole being was focussed on them, although I was also dimly aware of the palm of my hand pressing against the rough wall of the hotel bedroom.

As I took in that sensation, it transformed itself. The wall no longer formed a solid barrier. It was dissolving, had turned to light, and my arm was penetrating it. My hand could feel the cold of the street outside. Something, it may have been an insect, brushed past it. I panicked, thinking that the wall might solidify again around my forearm. I pulled it to me and held both arms out in front. A moment later my hands encountered another wall. Both were pressing against it and as before slowly sinking through it. But with horror I realised that it was not a wall. It was the ceiling. To ascertain this I twisted my whole body and indeed found myself looking down at the sleeping form of myself in the bed below. A fearful intimation of mortality, the chill and terrible hand of Death, seized my heart. I plunged downwards to repossess my body and the next moment was sitting bolt upright in bed, bathed in sweat and breathing heavily.

This was the first of a number of astral projections I have undergone since. I can now journey by day or night, and each time the journey takes me a little further. The mortal panic I experienced initially has been replaced curiously by a very strong sexual desire, and I now set off with the intention of encountering another travelling spirit and in the hope of re-enacting on the Astral Plane the scene set out in Mr Rollinson's wonderful poem.

Needless to say, Durian has dismissed these journeys as nothing more than dreams brought on by my overwrought and unstable condition. He is wrong. I am convinced that I have lived a previous existence in Cairo. It is a city to which my soul has returned after an absence of many millennia and is seeking out its old haunts. I was in the midst of exploring this fascinating notion when our stay was cut short by a disturbing event.

Just after dawn one morning, as we climbed the stairs to our room at the Hôtel du Nil, we heard an urgent knocking on one of the doors, then an angry voice saying, 'Open up, you dirty pervert bastards. I know you're in there.'

There was no mistaking the dulcet hacksaw tones. It was 'John' of Henderson's Debt Collection Agency. He was turning out to be a great deal more efficient than we had bargained for. The past was catching up with us.

Without a word, we climbed out of the bathroom window into an alleyway. We walked urgently out into the street and took a taxi straight to the airport.

TOKYO

It is not at all obvious how or why Lucan and Gray ended up in Tokyo. At no point in their writings do they express any desire to visit Japan, or mention any plan to do so, although this is to presuppose that they were working to some sort of itinerary, which they were not. In general, the only things that prompted them to move from one place to another were sudden impulse, boredom, or the sighting of an agent of Henderson's Debt Collection Agency.

It may be that they simply stopped off there en route to New Orleans. But, by all accounts, they spent a little over a fortnight in Japan, which suggests that it was more than just a stopover. Be that as it may, once they had arrived in the Japanese capital, they did plan at least one excursion: to follow in the footsteps of Lafcadio Hearn to Kaka, in the south-western corner of Honshu. Hearn was a 19th century American writer who went to live in Japan and opened up many aspects of Japanese life to the West. He also re-introduced to the Japanese themselves certain neglected aspects of their own culture. Lucan and Gray found a description of Hearn's intriguing voyage in his book, **Glimpses of Unfamiliar Japan**, which appeared in 1894. Part of this description is included below.

The material in this chapter has been taken directly from Durian Gray's 'diary'. This term is used very loosely. The word would normally imply some sort of correlation between the date on the page and the day on which the events took place. In the case of Gray's diary such an assumption would be simplistic in the extreme. The following may have been written while the two of them were on their way to Kaka. Or it may even have been written before they left.

*   *   *

## 28TH JULY

—⊃•◯•⊂—

After a long delay in Jakarta, where Medlar's collection of Indian wooden dildoes was impounded on the grounds that they constituted offensive weapons, we arrived at last in Tokyo. It was late, and the taxi driver was doubtful about finding us a hotel.

'All full,' he said.

'Why?'

'Many people sleeping.'

It was an ingenious explanation.

'Is there anywhere without people sleeping?'

He thought for a moment, then had a bright idea. 'Only Happy Ranch'.

'OK. Take us there.'

From the outside it looked ludicrous enough – a massive square building with a number of phallic towers clinging to the sides. A grinning neon cowboy and cowgirl adorned the façade. 'Albert Speer meets Walt Disney' is how Medlar described it. 'Florid and debased' were my epithets. And, as 'florid and debased' is a state to which all Decadent travellers should constantly aspire, we decided to check in.

The foyer was remarkably cramped for such a large building. We looked in vain for a reception desk. There was not a clerk, commissionaire or bellhop in sight. Several couples hurried past looking furtive. None would stop to explain how one went about finding a bed for the night. I wondered if they might not have been put off by the solar topee which Medlar had bought in Kuala Lumpur and had insisted on wearing ever since. Eventually a couple arrived who proved more compliant. The man pointed to two illuminated numbers on an electronic display board and went towards the stairs beckoning us to follow.

On the first floor we watched as the man inserted several yen notes into a slot in the bedroom door until it finally flew open. He then pointed to the door adjacent. We followed suit, and stepped into a room whose chief quality – whose only quality – was that of hygiene. Other than that it was small and garish – reminding us strongly of the Queen Mother.

There was the obligatory television screen, this one of cinematic proportions, which displayed an unending stream of torrid pornographic films. There was also a loudspeaker system from which emanated a selection of execrable music and such bizarre sounds as gongs, crowing cocks and the ambient sound of a railway station. Medlar of course found the railway noises highly arousing.

I lay down on my bed and a deep melancholy flooded my soul. I was expecting to be surrounded by blood-red lacquer furniture, tatami screens and brisk, fond geishas, gorgeously attired, attending to me with a mixture of modesty and smouldering sensuality. Instead, here I was surrounded by plastic and the vocal displays of several varieties of cock.

'Do you think we have to pay to leave this place as well?' I asked Medlar.

'A good deal more than it cost us to get in, I shouldn't wonder.' He was looking even more melancholy than I was.

Not wishing to spend any more time than was absolutely necessary in the hotel room, we went out in search of some diversion. We wandered the Yoshiwara area of the city, but knowing no Japanese, we had little idea of what services were on offer. Eventually we chose to let the finger of fate decide. We stepped off the street, through a bead curtain and into a small, smoky room.

We stopped just inside the door. It took a moment or two for our eyes to become accustomed to the light. We were about to move further inside when an arm appeared from the darkness barring our way. A Japanese man of Sumo proportions held out a bunch of tickets. He spread them out in a fan like a magician doing a card trick, then held them up to his face. He tilted his large head to one side and cast his gaze downwards with a look of the utmost maidenly modesty. When he removed the fan from in front of his face again, he had a wide grin which revealed the rotten stumps of his teeth, visible even in that dim light.

We were delighted by his performance, smiled at him in an appreciative manner and moved on. This time the arm grabbed me and held me tight. The smile was replaced by a look of menace and the man was talking with remarkable speed. I looked at Medlar who looked at me and shrugged his shoulders. We were rescued by an American in a business suit who explained that we were expected to buy a ticket. We asked him if it was worth it and he said, on balance, it probably was.

In the pale glow which came from a spotlight we could see a

small square stage which projected into the room. Behind it was a long red curtain with tatami screens either side of it. There were two or three rows of seating around three sides of the stage. The rest of the space was empty – standing room. The seats were sparsely occupied by a number of men who had the air of regular customers. They had an air of eager anticipation, rather than furtiveness, about them. Others stood around in the space behind the seats. I, Medlar and our American friend stood a little distance from the stage with our backs to the wall. For the first time I noticed music – the silk strings of the traditional Japanese koto – playing quietly in the background.

After a short time, the curtain parted and the gigantic ticket seller re-appeared. By the time he had lumbered awkwardly into the spotlight, it was shining with much greater intensity. However the ceiling was low and the man was so wide that only his head and a strip down the middle of his body was illuminated. He was wearing a mask – that of a wrinkled old man with two small horns on top of his head. It was obviously a character from a Noh play, although neither Medlar nor I understood the precise significance of this. The majority of the audience on the other hand understood the humour of the reference. They clapped and laughed. From behind the mask came his muffled voice which the American was good enough to translate for us.

'He's telling us who's performing tonight. They were hoping for a Black American dancer, but she got a better offer. Akikochan is back after a very successful tour of naval bases in the South Pacific . . .'

There was some polite applause at this point. We joined in, feigning connoisseurship. Medlar said that if he had known the artistes were of international stature, he would have dressed more formally.

'. . . he's now introducing the star of the show who will surely meet with the fervent approval of this honourable and distinguished audience.'

The wrestler turned and ambled back to the curtain. He took a moment to find the opening before he disappeared behind it. The lights went down. The sense of anticipation and the volume of the music increased. But this time it was accompanied by a woman's voice which was coming from behind the curtain, singing what sounded like a traditional and rather melancholic folk song well-suited to the plangent sounds of the koto.

Our American gave us a whispered explanation. The words, he said, tell the tale of a young woman whose lover has returned to his wife and family after spending a few short but passionate hours with her. She sits alone in her empty room, not knowing how long she will have to wait before she sees him again or indeed if she will ever see him again.

Slowly, the curtains parted and a woman appeared. At first all we could make out was the white oval of her face, the vermilion curve of her lips and the thin black semicircles of her eyebrows. She was wearing a sumptuous kimono, the same deep red as the curtain, so that she appeared to be no more than a floating head. As she came forward and, as it were, separated out from her background, she took on the very incarnation of the spirit of the music. She walked forward as if weighed down both by her gorgeous attire and the deeply-felt grief she was expressing through the words of her song. One of the men in the seats stood up for a moment, perhaps in defiance of this image that confronted him. Then he sank back down into his seat again as if defeated and overwhelmed by the beauty and sorrow of this creature. From the rapt attention of the audience I surmised that this was Akiko-chan.

She began to dance in a distracted way. The spotlight above her had been dimmed and she was now bathed in a gentle light from the side. Her dancing had very little of the fluid about it. Her movements were tight and cramped. Longing wracked her body. She sank to her knees and began to sing again. The American continued his translation:

'The girl's looking out at the autumn leaves falling from the peach tree in the courtyard. The tree will soon be as empty as her heart.'

The upper folds of Akiko-chan's kimono were loosened as she knelt on the stage and one side began to slip off her shoulder. She did not notice at first. Then, with a gesture of flustered modesty, she hurriedly rearranged her attire. In her haste she revealed a momentary glimpse of her small firm breasts.

From the kneeling position she had slumped sideways, supporting her body on her left hand. She returned to her song. As the girl was remembering the tenderness of her recently-departed lover, Akiko-chan's right hand began to seek out the opening of her kimono and, having found it, began to stray beneath its folds. At the same time she moved her right leg backwards to reveal more of the opening, through which her bare calves were now visible.

Some of the men in the seats were beginning to get agitated, shifting their positions to catch a glimpse of something which was probably not visible. Others were transfixed, entranced by what they were witnessing. One elder man in the seats opposite us was sitting with head tilted up and tears streaming down his cheeks. As far as Akiko-chan was concerned however, the audience did not exist. Her gaze was fixed on the peach tree in the courtyard and her hand was seeking out the place her lover had recently vacated. This continued for a few minutes before, still supporting herself on her left hand, her right hand unwound and removed the sash that went around the waist of her kimono. Now, as if finally overcome by the depth of her despair, she fell backwards onto the stage and lay there motionless for some time.

A concerned muttering filled the room. One or two of the audience looked at each other and smiled nervously. Almost imperceptibly one of the little feet encased in white cotton socks began to rise. It slowly lifted off the floor of the stage, getting higher and higher. An audible sigh – of wonderment and desire – also rose from the men at the front closest to Akiko-chan's body lying prone a few feet from them. The silk of her kimono began to slide along her leg as she raised her foot higher. Then at a certain point she bent her knee and brought it down to touch her chest. Maintaining this position she slowly rotated her body left and right so that she could be scrutinised from all corners of the room. The collective sigh now gave way to something closer to a gasp and some of those standing followed the line of the singer's body as it moved back and forth.

The attention of the audience suddenly shifted, as the curtain opened again and the ticket-seller, minus his mask, appeared and stood to one side of the stage. Again, without seeming to notice the presence of any others, Akiko-chan lifted herself back into the kneeling position. Her kimono was loose and her black hair was falling in disarray about her ears and neck. From nowhere she produced a small lacquer box and took out what looked like contraceptive sheaths – four or five of them – wrapped in silver foil. She used her teeth to tear off the wrapping, then remained where she was, eyes downcast, as demure and modest as a subservient daughter, waiting for a signal. Several members of the audience sitting in the front row raised their index fingers. After a short period, the singer lifted her gaze and surveyed the collection of upraised fingers in front of her. She had distributed four of the contraceptives when, on a whim, I stepped forward out of the darkness and caught her attention. She looked at me slightly startled for a moment, as if she recognised me. Then she beckoned me forward.

I made my way through the chairs and stood in front of the stage, facing her. She gathered her kimono about her, then took hold of my hand and found my index finger. She straightened it and expertly rolled the final contraceptive onto it. Still holding my finger, she leant back, supported herself on her other hand and parted her thighs to reveal a partially shaven pubis. She guided my finger towards her vagina and after she had used it to circle her clitoris, she eased it between the soft folds. With a little squirm she caused it to disappear inside her.

I looked up at her face. Beneath the white powder, the exquisitely applied eyebrows and the lip paint, I saw a face worn out by years of debauchery. The breasts, which from a distance looked firm, were not in fact those of a young woman. Her beauty was corrupt – which made her all the more beautiful in my eyes. I detected a faint smile as of complicity at the corner of her mouth and realised that hers was not the history of a victim, but of a debauchee. I read in her eyes the look of someone who was doing this not because she had to make money, but because she was compelled to by her own demons.

I could feel the internal landscape of her sex as she moved around on my finger. The sensation was not unlike that of feeling for giblets inside the carcass of a quail. Then, as if a bell had

111

silently rung, signalling my time was up, she withdrew from my finger and made me hold it up to the light. Her juices glistened on the rubber surface. She said something to me which I did not understand. Almost ritualistically, she removed the contraceptive, folded it carefully in a piece of tissue paper and placed it in the lacquer box. She looked past me, seeking out the next of the chosen. Her face had resumed its blank loveliness.

The next four took their turns. One of them tried drunkenly to insert two fingers and was chastised for his presumption. She called forward the wrestler and the man withdrew hastily, bowing to both the singer and the sumo.

A young man who had watched Akiko-chan throughout, with a look of veneration on his face, came forward. He stumbled as he approached the stage, his hand shaking so that Akiko-chan had difficulty placing the contraceptive on his finger. Suddenly she stopped and looked at the young man intently. A shudder ran though his body. Then he bowed and turned away, convulsed with shame and confusion.

Akiko-chan stood up, gathering the folds of her kimono around her, and tied it with the sash that lay at her feet. The wrestler came forward, made an announcement and, after a gesture in the direction of Akiko-chan, began the applause. By the time we joined in, she had already left the stage.

## 6TH AUGUST

———◦◒◦———

As we left the hotel this morning, we were struck anew by the furtive behaviour of the other guests. We concluded that the place must be an 'adulterers' safe house'. Medlar was amused at the thought. I, however, felt demeaned, tainted and disgusted. Not morally, of course, but aesthetically.

Medlar could not see what I objected to. I attempted to explain. 'To me there is something irredeemably ugly about the bourgeois notion of sin. It's so petty, so narrow.'

'I couldn't agree more. So when they break out of it for a night of passion in a plastic box, it's rather touching, isn't it?'

'Not at all. I find it repellent.'

'You surprise me, dear Durian. You're usually such a stout defender of the right to copulate.'

'And so I remain. It's not the copulation that I object to, but the state of mind in which it's done.'

'How on earth do you presume to know that?'

'By the looks on their faces.'

'Have you seen them at it?' He became excited at the thought. 'When? How?'

'No, no. I mean afterwards. In the foyer. How they creep and scurry.'

'Don't they just!'

'I doubt if there's a single couple in this entire Temple of Penetration that isn't squirming with guilt and anxiety.'

Medlar pondered this for a few moments.

'You've obviously thought about all this in a great deal more detail than I have,' he said in his gravest and most magisterial manner. 'I have to admit you're right. It's a revolting spectacle. We must put clear blue water between ourselves and The Happy Ranch as soon as possible.'

'Are you suggesting it's time to visit the Cave of the Ghostly Children?'

'I think I very probably am.'


We made for the underground. Our aim was Ueno station, where we would catch a bullet train to Matsue, then a bus – or possibly a light aircraft – to Kaka, with further transport arrangements to be finalised when we arrived.

As we were carried along in the tidal wave, or tsunami, of Tokyo commuters, I began to feel uneasy. Tokyo's reputation for being enormously crowded is thoroughly deserved, although the Decadent traveller need not necessarily be repelled by this. Indeed for the true Decadent, as our beloved Baudelaire pointed out,

*To enjoy the crowd is an art. And this can create, at the expense of humankind, a drunken excess of vitality in one who has had instilled in him from his earliest days a taste for transgression and mask, hatred of the domestic and a passion for travel.*

*Multitude, solitude – equal and interchangeable terms for the poet with an active, fertile mind. He who does not know how to people his solitude is equally incapable of being alone in a busy crowd.*

*. . . He who loses himself in a crowd knows the fervent delights which will always elude egoists, closed up like coffers, or idlers, withdrawn like snails.*

Even so, when one is travelling on the Tokyo underground, assailed on all sides by a fetid, heaving. stinking mass of human-ity, with one's nose squashed into a commuter's ear, it requires an almost superhuman effort of will and imagination to feel oneself alone or indeed to experience anything resembling 'fervent delights'.

The Tokyo system is clean, bright and efficient – qualities which neither of us find attractive. We greatly prefer the subway of New York. At least that still has the capacity to inspire some of the ancient terrors associated with a journey underground. In New York, it really is necessary to abandon all hope as you des-cend the escalator to ride the satanic, graffiti-daubed trains through the hellish regions beyond Manhattan – risking robbery, wounding or gang rape, especially if, like us, you deliberately choose to ride them late at night. But Tokyo has its pleasures too.

Once below ground, travellers are packed into carriages by men in uniform wearing white gloves. At the sight of these men my heart started palpitating like a young girl's. I was immedi-ately transported back to my days at the military academy in Bogotá where my father sent me at the age of twelve. He had taken this course of action on the grounds that, in the time-honoured way, it would make a man of me. Dear, sweet, foolish man! Little did he know that this was akin to sending Casanova to a nunnery to make a good Christian of him. Ah, how I loved the ethos of the academy, especially those random acts of savage discipline which were so much part of everyday life there. These acts, more often than not, were perpetrated by young men in tight-fitting uniforms and white gloves. But in the aftermath of these bouts of perverse cruelty came an even greater pleasure – the cloyingly sentimental consolation which one found in the arms of one's fellow-cadets. It was a heady concoction. They really are the best days of one's life. It was all too beautiful to last, of course. I was sent home after two terms – the only cadet ever to be expelled from the San Miguel Academy for enjoying it 'to an unhealthy degree'.

When I had recovered my strength sufficiently, I allowed myself to be squeezed into a carriage. It was like entering a mangle. I must have exchanged germs with at least three hundred people. As the train accelerated along the tracks, our bodies were flung together and tumbled about until we were a single homogeneous mass of sweat-soaked, joggling flesh. At one point, I managed with difficulty to turn my head sufficiently to catch sight of Medlar with a most lascivious smile on his face. Just in front of him was a middle-aged gentleman who was pressed up closely against a schoolgirl modestly dressed in a navy blue suit. It took no time to realise what was causing the smile on Medlar's face. The gentleman was groping the schoolgirl, and Medlar – whether in a spirit of satire, sympathy or revenge I could not tell – was groping the gentleman.

The cult of the schoolgirl is one of the more impenetrable aspects of Japan. On our way to the underground we had come across a shop which specialised in the sale of used scholastic underwear. Little feminine stains, broken elastic or a trapped curl of pubic hair raise the price of an item considerably. It appears that selling their knickers allows girls to make extra pocket money in this heavily consumerist society. One can only admire their spirit of enterprise. Our Victorian forebears would certainly have approved.

It also appears that fondling schoolgirls in the subway is practically a national sport in Japan. A recent survey revealed that 75% of Tokyo girls between 13 and 18 have experienced this form of involuntary massage. The government has only just made it illegal to procure sex from teenagers and younger girls. Apparently, one of the first to be arrested under that law was a senior civil servant.

But to return to the underground carriage. By now Medlar had lost interest in the gentleman in front. He had turned away and was staring intently at a comic book. It was being read by a respectable, elderly, besuited man in the seat to Medlar's right. The image he happened to be scrutinising at that moment was of a young girl with impossibly large eyes and purple hair lying bound hand and foot in the coils of a vivid red alien creature of a reptilian sort. She was wearing a tartan skirt pulled up around her waist and a somewhat surprised expression on her face as the alien reptile used its tentacles to penetrate her vaginally, anally and orally simultaneously. Medlar drew my attention to the image, and I remarked on how very different this comic was from a good old Rupert Bear annual.

However, at the same time, a wistful sigh welled up inside me. I was struck by a sudden mood of tristesse as I realised what the image brought to mind. *The Dream of the Fisherman's Wife*. In this, one of the most extraordinary of all Japanese 'shunga' a naked woman lies on rocks covered with green seaweed in the tentacles of two octopuses. She swoons with pleasure as an enormous octopus with terrifying eyes sucks greedily at her vulva, and the smaller octopus embraces her mouth.

*The Dream of the Fisherman's Wife* was one of a number of rare erotic Japanese drawings and prints we had collected over the years. It was the work of Utamaro, a master of colour, rhythm and line, whose harmonies of red, blue, orange and green exquisitely complement the flowing lines of the figures, especially their enlarged and elaborated genitals. Writing of Utamaro, Edmond de Goncourt refers to '. . . *the fiery passions of the copulations he depicted . . . those swooning women, their heads uptilted on the ground, their faces death-like, their eyes closed beneath painted eye-lids; that strength amid power of delineation that make the drawing of a penis equal to that of a hand in the Louvre museum attributed to Michelangelo.*'

I was contrasting in my mind the beauty of our collection of erotic drawings with what we now saw before us. That contrast seemed to encapsulate the metamorphosis which Japanese culture has undergone, replacing exquisite refinement in everything from Art to Cruelty with a crude democratic vulgarity. No wonder our dear friend Yukio Mishima felt compelled to disembowel himself as a mark of protest – a gesture rendered even more beautiful by virtue of its total futility and inefficacy.

Medlar suggested that the image of an innocent young Japanese girl being entered in her anus, vagina and mouth by a huge repulsive alien may have been intended as an allegory of the effect of American culture on post-war Japan. I thought this a very pretty hypothesis.

Medlar drew further comparisons with the work of Sadao Hasegawa. In particular he saw the influence of such paintings as *Human Candlestick, The Long-nosed Goblin from Kurama* and *Joyfully Seeking the Impure Land*. But I was unconvinced by this – Hasegawa's work is exclusively homo-erotic after all . . .

While this heated debate continued, the Japanese reader turned to his fellow-travellers and smiled. He rose from his seat, bowed his head quickly several times and left, the very model of gentleness and good manners.

We were left high and dry, reflecting nostalgically not only on the collection of shunga we had to leave behind in Edinburgh, but everything else we lost in that cataclysm too . . .

The underground train was still moving cleanly and quietly towards Ueno station. At a certain stop, large numbers of travellers got off, and I found a seat. To prepare myself for the coming adventure, I took out my copy of Lafcadio Hearn's *Glimpses of Unfamiliar Japan*. I began to read.

### I

*It is forbidden to go to Kaka if there be wind enough 'to move three hairs.' Now an absolutely windless day is rare on this wild western coast. Over the Japanese Sea, from Korea, or China, or boreal Siberia, some west or northwest breeze is nearly always blowing. So that I have had to wait many long months for a good chance to visit Kaka.*

*Taking the shortest route, one goes first to Mitsu-ura from Matsue, either by kuruma or on foot. By kuruma this little journey occupies nearly two hours and a half, though the distance is scarcely seven miles, the road being one of the worst in all Izumo. You leave Matsue to enter at once into a broad plain, level as a lake, all occupied by rice-fields and walled in by wooded hills. The path, barely wide enough for a single vehicle, traverses this green desolation, climbs the heights beyond it, and* descends again into another and a larger level of rice-fields, surrounded also by hills. The path over the second line of hills is much steeper; then a third rice-plain must be crossed and a third chain of green altitudes, lofty enough to merit the name of mountains. Of course one must make the ascent on foot: it is no small labour for a kurumaya to pull even an empty kuruma up to the top; and how he manages to do so without breaking the little vehicle is a mystery for the path is stony and rough as the bed of a torrent. A tiresome climb I find it; but the landscape view from the summit is more than compensation.

Then descending, there remains a fourth and last wide level of rice-fields to traverse. The absolute flatness of the great plains between the ranges, and the singular way in which these latter 'fence off' the country into sections, are matters for surprise even in a land of surprises like Japan. Beyond the fourth rice-valley there is a fourth hill chain, lower and richly wooded, on reaching the base of which the traveller must finally abandon his kuruma, and proceed over the hills on foot. Behind them lies the sea. But the very worst bit of the journey now begins. The path makes an easy winding ascent between bamboo growths and young pine and other vegetation for a shaded quarter of a mile, passing before various little shrines and pretty homesteads surrounded by high-hedged gardens. Then it suddenly breaks into steps, or rather ruins of steps – partly hewn in the rock, partly built, everywhere breached and worn – which descend, all edge-less, in a manner amazingly precipitous, to the village of Mitsu-ura. With straw sandals, which never slip, the country folk can nimbly hurry up or down such a path; but with foreign footgear one slips at nearly every step; and when you reach the bottom at last, the wonder of how you managed to get there, even with the assistance of your faithful kurumaya, keeps you for a moment quite unconscious of the fact that you are already in Mitsu-ura.

## II

Mitsu-ura stands with its back to the mountains, at the end of a small deep bay hemmed in by very high cliffs. There is only one narrow strip of beach at the foot of the heights; and the village owes its existence to that fact, for beaches are rare on this part of the coast. Crowded between the cliffs and the sea, the houses have a painfully compressed aspect, and somehow the greater number give one the impression of things created out of wrecks of junks. The little streets, or rather alleys, are full of boats

and skeletons of boats and boat timbers; and every where, suspended
from bamboo poles much taller than the houses, immense bright brown
fishing-nets are drying in the sun. The whole curve of the beach is also
lined with boats, lying side by side, so that I wonder how it will be
possible to get to the water's edge without climbing over them. There is
no hotel; but I find hospitality in a fisherman's dwelling, while my
kurumaya goes somewhere to hire a boat for Kaka-ura.

In less than ten minutes there is a crowd of several hundred people
about the house, half-clad adults and perfectly naked boys. They block-
ade the building; they obscure the light by filling up the doorways and
climbing into the windows to look at the foreigner. The aged proprietor
of the cottage protests in vain, says harsh things; the crowd only
thickens. Then all the sliding screens are closed. But in the paper panes
there are holes; and at all the lower holes the curious take regular
turns at peeping. At a higher hole I do some peeping myself. The
crowd is not prepossessing: it is squalid, dull-featured, remarkably
ugly. But it is gentle and silent; and there are one or two pretty faces
in it which seem extraordinary by reason of the general homeliness of
the rest.

At last my kurumaya has succeeded in making arrangements for a
boat; and I effect a sortie to the beach, followed by the kurumaya and by
all my besiegers. Boats have been moved to make a passage for us, and
we embark without trouble of any sort. Our crew consists of two
scullers, – an old man at the stern, wearing only a rokushaku about his
loins, and an old woman at the bow, fully robed and wearing an
immense straw hat shaped like a mushroom. Both of course stand to
their work and it would be hard to say which is the stronger or more
skilful sculler. We passengers squat Oriental fashion upon a mat in the
centre of the boat, where a hibachi, well stocked with glowing charcoal,
invites us to smoke.

### III

The day is clear blue to the end of the world, with a faint wind from the
east, barely enough to wrinkle the sea, certainly more than enough to
move three hairs. Nevertheless the boatwoman and the boatman do not
seem anxious; and I begin to wonder whether the famous prohibition is
not a myth. So delightful the transparent water looks, that before we
have left the bay I have to yield to its temptation by plunging in and

swimming after the boat. When I climb back on board we are rounding the promontory on the right; and the little vessel begins to rock. Even under this thin wind the sea is moving in long swells. And as we pass into the open, following the westward trend of the land, we find ourselves gliding over an ink-black depth, in front of one of the very grimmest coasts I ever saw.

A tremendous line of dark iron-coloured cliffs, towering sheer from the sea without a beach, and with never a speck of green below their summits; and here and there along this terrible front, monstrous beetlings, breaches, fissures, earthquake rendings, and topplings-down. Enormous fractures show lines of strata pitched up skyward, or plunging down into the ocean with the long fall of cubic miles of cliff. Before fantastic gaps, prodigious masses of rock, of all nightmarish shapes, rise from profundities unfathomed. And though the wind to-day seems trying to hold its breath, white breakers are reaching far up the cliffs, and dashing their foam into the faces of the splintered crags. We are too far to hear the thunder of them; but their ominous sheet-lightning fully explains to me the story of the three hairs. Along this goblin coast on a wild day there would be no possible chance for the strongest swimmer or the stoutest boat; there is no place for the foot, no hold for the hand, nothing but the sea raving against a precipice of iron. Even to-day, under the feeblest breath imaginable, great swells deluge us with spray as they splash past. And for two long hours this jagged frowning coast towers by; and, as we toil on, rocks rise around us like black teeth; and always, far away, the foam-bursts gleam at the feet of the implacable cliffs. But there are no sounds save the lapping and plashing of passing swells, and the monotonous creaking of the sculls upon their pegs of wood.

At last, at last, a bay, – a beautiful large bay, with a demilune of soft green hills about it, overtopped by far blue mountains, – and in the very farthest point of the bay a miniature village, in front of which many junks are riding at anchor: Kaka-ura. But we do not go to Kaka-ura yet; the Kukedo are not there. We cross the broad opening of the bay, journey along another half mile of ghastly sea-precipice, and finally make for a lofty promontory of naked Plutonic rock. We pass by its menacing foot, slip along its side, and lo! at an angle opens the arched mouth of a wonderful cavern, broad, lofty, and full of light, with no floor but the sea. Beneath us, as we slip into it, I can see rocks fully twenty feet down. The water is clear as air. This is the Shin-Kukedo, called the New

Cavern, though assuredly older than human record by a hundred thousand years.

## IV

A more beautiful sea-cave could scarcely be imagined. The sea, tunnelling the tall promontory through and through, has also, like a great architect, ribbed and groined and polished its mighty work. The arch of the entrance is certainly twenty feet above the deep water, and fifteen wide; and trillions of wave tongues have licked the vault and walls into wondrous smoothness. As we proceed, the rock-roof steadily heightens and the way widens. Then we unexpectedly glide under a heavy shower of fresh water, dripping from overhead. This spring is called the o-chozubachi or mitarashi of Shin-Kukedo-San.

Such are the names given to the water-vessels or cisterns at which Shinto worshipers must wash their hands and rinse their mouths ere praying to the Kami. A mitarashi or o-chozubachi is placed before every Shinto temple. The pilgrim to Shin-Kukedo-San should perform this ceremonial ablution at the little rockspring above described, before entering the sacred cave. Here even the gods of the cave are said to wash after having passed through the sea water.

From the high vault at this point it is believed that a great stone will detach itself and fall upon any evil-hearted person who should attempt to enter the cave. I safely pass through the ordeal.

Suddenly as we advance the boatwoman takes a stone from the bottom of the boat, and with it begins to rap heavily on the bow; and the hollow echoing is reiterated with thundering repercussions through all the cave. And in another instant we pass into a great burst of light, coming from the mouth of a magnificent and lofty archway on the left, opening into the cavern at right angles. This explains the singular illumination of the long vault, which at first seemed to come from beneath; for while the opening was still invisible all the water appeared to be suffused with light. Through this grand arch, between outlying rocks, a strip of beautiful green undulating coast appears, over miles of azure water. We glide on toward the third entrance to the Kukedo, opposite to that by which we came in; and enter the dwelling-place of the Kami and the Hotoke, for this grotto is sacred both to Shinto and to Buddhist faith. Here the Kukedo reaches its greatest altitude and breadth. Its vault is fully forty feet above the water, and its walls thirty feet apart. Far up on the right, near the roof, is a projecting white rock, and above the rock an orifice wherefrom a slow stream drips, seeming white as the rock itself.

This is the legendary Fountain of Jizo, the fountain of milk at which the souls of dead children drink. Sometimes it flows more swiftly, sometime more slowly; but it never ceases by night or day And mothers suffering from want of milk come hither to pray that milk may be given unto them and their prayer is heard. And mothers having more milk than their infants need come hither also and pray to Jizo that so much as they can give may be taken for the dead children; and their prayer is heard, and their milk diminishes.

At least thus the peasants of Izumo say.

And the echoing of the swells leaping against the rocks without the rushing and rippling of the tide against the walls, the heavy rain of percolating water, sounds of lapping and gurgling and plashing, and sounds of mysterious origin coming from no visible where, make it difficult for us to hear each other speak. The cavern seems full of voices, as if a host of invisible beings were holding tumultuous converse.

Below us all the deeply lying rocks are naked to view as if seen through glass. It seems to me that nothing could be more delightful than to swim through this cave and let one's self drift with the sea-currents through all its cool shadows. But as I am on the point of jumping in, all the other occupants of the boat utter wild cries of protest. It is certain death! men who jumped in here only six months ago were never heard of again! this is sacred water, Kami-noumi! And as if to conjure away my temptation, the boatwoman again seizes her little stone and raps fearfully upon the bow. On finding, however, that I am not sufficiently deterred by these stories of sudden death and disappearance, she suddenly screams into my ear the magic word,

'SAMÉ.'

Sharks! I have no longer any desire whatever to swim through the many-sounding halls of Shin-Kukedo-San. I have lived in the tropics!

And we start forthwith for Kyu-Kukedo-San, the Ancient Cavern.

## V

For the ghastly fancies about the Kami-noumi, the word 'samé' afforded a satisfactory explanation. But why that long, loud, weird rapping on the bow with a stone evidently kept on board for no other purpose? There was an exaggerated earnestness about the action which gave me *an uncanny sensation, something like that which moves a man while walking at night upon a lonesome road, full of queer shadows, to sing at the top of his voice. The boatwoman at first declares that the rapping was made only for the sake of the singular echo. But after some cautious further questioning, I discover a much more sinister reason for the performance. Moreover, I learn that all the seamen and seawomen of this coast do the same thing when passing through perilous places, or places believed to be haunted by the Ma. What are the Ma?*

*Goblins!*

## VI

*From the caves of the Kami we retrace our course for about a quarter of a mile; then make directly for an immense perpendicular wrinkle in the long line of black cliffs. Immediately before it a huge dark rock towers from the sea, whipped by the foam of breaking swells. Rounding it, we glide behind it into still water and shadow, the shadow of a monstrous cleft in the precipice of the coast. And suddenly, at an unsuspected angle, the mouth of another cavern yawns before us; and in another moment our boat touches its threshold of stone with a little shock that sends a long sonorous echo, like the sound of a temple drum, booming through all the abysmal place. A single glance tells me whither we have come. Far within the dusk I see the face of a Jizo, smiling in pale stone, and before him, and all about him, a weird congregation of gray shapes without shape, a host of fantasticalities that strangely suggest the wreck of a cemetery. From the sea the ribbed floor of the cavern slopes high through deepening shadows back to the black mouth of a farther grotto; and all that slope is covered with hundreds and thousands of forms like shattered haka. But as the eyes grow accustomed to the gloaming it becomes manifest that these were never haka; they are only little towers of stone and pebbles deftly piled up by long and patient labour.*

*'Shinda kodomo no shigoto,' my kurumaya murmurs with a compassionate smile; 'all this is the work of the dead children.'*

*And we disembark. By counsel, I take off my shoes and put on a pair of zori, or straw sandals provided for me, as the rock is extremely slippery. The others land barefoot. But how to proceed soon becomes a puzzle: the countless stone-piles stand so close together that no space for the foot seems to be left between them.*

*'Mada mihki ga arimasu!'* the boatwoman announces, leading the way. There is a path.

Following after her, we squeeze ourselves between the wall of the cavern on the right and some large rocks, and discover a very, very narrow passage left open between the stone-towers. But we are warned to be careful for the sake of the little ghosts: if any of their work be overturned, they will cry. So we move very cautiously and slowly across the cave to a space bare of stone-heaps, where the rocky floor is covered with a thin layer of sand, detritus of a crumbling ledge above it. And in that sand I see light prints of little feet, children's feet, tiny naked feet, only three or four inches long, – the footprints of the infant ghosts.

Had we come earlier, the boatwoman says, we should have seen many more. For 't is at night, when the soil of the cavern is moist with dews and drippings from the roof, that they leave their footprints upon it; but when the heat of the day comes, and the sand and the rocks dry up, the prints of the little feet vanish away.

There are only three footprints visible, but these are singularly distinct. One points toward the wall of the cavern; the others toward the sea. Here and there upon ledges or projections of the rock, all about the cavern, tiny straw sandals – children's zori are lying: offerings of pilgrims to the little ones, that their feet may not be wounded by the stones. But all the ghostly footprints are prints of naked feet

Then we advance, picking our way very, very carefully between the stone-towers, toward the mouth of the inner grotto, and reach the statue of Jizo before it.

A seated Jizo, carven in granite, holding in one hand the mystic jewel by virtue of which all wishes may be fulfilled; in the other his shakujo, or pilgrim's staff. Before him (strange condescension of Shinto faith!) a little torii has been erected, and a pair of gohei! Evidently this gentle divinity has no enemies; at the feet of the lover of children's ghosts, both creeds unite in tender homage.

I said feet. But this subterranean Jizo has only one foot. The carven lotus on which he reposes has been fractured and broken: two great petals are missing; and the right foot, which must have rested upon one of them, has been knocked off at the ankle. This, I learn upon inquiry, has been done by the waves. In times of great storm the billows rush into the cavern like raging Oni, and sweep all the little stone towers into shingle as they come, and dash the statues against the rocks. But always during the first still night after the tempest the work is reconstructed as before!

'Hotoke ga shimpai shite; naki-naki tsumi naoshimasu.' They make mourning, the hotoke; weeping, they pile up the stones again, they rebuild their towers of prayer.

All about the black mouth of the inner grotto the bone-colored rock bears some resemblance to a vast pair of yawning jaws. Downward from this sinister portal the cavern-floor slopes into a deeper and darker aperture. And within it, as one's eyes become accustomed to the gloom, a still larger vision of stone towers is disclosed; and beyond them, in a nook of the grotto, three other statues of Jizo smile, each one with a torii, before it. Here I have the misfortune to upset first one stone-pile and then another, while trying to, proceed. My kurumaya, almost simultaneously, ruins a third. To atone therefor, we must build six new towers, or double the number of those which we have cast down. And while we are thus busied, the boatwoman tells of two fishermen who remained in the cavern through all one night, and heard the humming of the viewless gathering, and sounds of speech, like the speech of children murmuring in multitude.

## VII

Only at night do the shadowy children come to build their little stone-heaps at the feet of Jizo; and it is said that every night the stones are changed. When I ask why they do not work by day, when there is none to see them, I am answered: 'O-Hi-San might see them; the dead exceedingly fear the Lady-Sun.'

To the question, 'Why do they come from the sea?' I can get no satisfactory answer. But doubtless in the quaint imagination of this people, as also in that of many another, there lingers still the primitive idea of some communication, mysterious and awful, between the world of waters and the world of the dead. It is always over the sea, after the Feast of Souls, that the spirits pass murmuring back to their dim realm, in those elfish little ships of straw which are launched for them upon the sixteenth day of the seventh moon. Even where these are launched upon rivers, or when floating lanterns are set adrift upon lakes or canals to light the ghosts upon their way, or when a mother bereaved drops into some running stream one hundred little prints of Jizo for the sake of her *lost darling, the vague idea behind the pious act is that all waters flow to the sea and the sea itself unto the 'Nether-distant Land.'*

*Some time, somewhere, this day will come back to me at night, with its visions and sounds: the dusky cavern, and its gray hosts of stone climbing back into darkness, and the faint prints of little naked feet, and the weirdly smiling images, and the broken syllables of the waters, inward-borne, multiplied by husky echoings, blending into one vast ghostly whispering, like the humming of the Sai-no-Kawara.*

*And over the black-blue bay we glide to the rocky beach of Kaka-ura.'*

\*    \*    \*

[Editors' Note] The diary entry comes to a halt at this point. In the event, Lucan and Gray never quite succeeded in making the journey they had set their hearts on. Intent on taking the train from Tokyo central station to Matsue, by virtue of a combination of linguistic incompetence and the Japanese desire to please, they ended up getting out at the wrong stop and found themselves in Waterfront, a recent suburb of Tokyo which was constructed on a vast accumulation of the city's garbage. When Lucan and Gray discovered this, they were delighted, convinced that they could sense the decay and corruption under their very feet.

Several hours later they were found lying side by side in the cement dust of an unfinished apartment building. They were surrounded by small piles of bricks and in a state of unconsciousness brought on by a mixture of Suntory and amphetamines. They were wrapped in each others arms, smiling beatifically, like the ghosts of small children. They had lost or been relieved of whatever money and valuables they had had about their persons.

# NEW ORLEANS

One very important principle of Decadent travel is that one should rarely if ever have an itinerary or a goal. To be in possession of either is to expose oneself to the pox of the package holiday, to join the ever-swelling ranks of petty-bourgeois tourists who believe that getting a dose of sunstroke beside a vulgar swimming pool in the Caribbean is the height of sophistication.

This does not mean that the Decadent traveller is not guided by certain principles. Indeed Medlar and I have formulated two. The first principle by which to judge whether a city is worth visiting or not is, naturally, the degree of perversion and depravity one might expect to find there, although, as Medlar pointed out, the very act of our visiting a city inevitably brings about a steep rise in the level of perversion and depravity. When it came to deciding whether to visit New Orleans, for example, this criterion was in doubt. Certainly its reputation as a City of Sin was formidable, and in some obscure way we have always felt an affinity with the place. New Orleans we considered as something of a spiritual home. We could feel its dark gravitational pull. Everything about it called out to the most sinister and dissolute aspects of our Decadent souls. At the same time, however, we were concerned about the extent to which our perception may have been distorted. The longer our exile continued, the more we realised how much we had previously lived in the company of books and, *quelle horreur!* how much the world out there failed to live up to the printed version.

The second principle of Decadent travel is to discover whether the city in question contains anybody who will entertain and accommodate one in an appropriately extravagant and lavish manner without expecting anything in return, especially gratitude. Medlar and I are of one mind where gratitude is concerned. It is simply the most base and pernicious of virtues. To express gratitude is a form of self-degradation to which I would never stoop – although there are numerous other forms of self-degradation to which I would readily stoop. Nor would I expect any friend worthy of the name to ask it of me. This is a very important dictum for the would-be Decadent traveller. Be thankful to nobody. The only useful function that gratitude performs is in the arena of revenge. To my mind, there is no more satisfying form of revenge than to make another feel grateful to you.

When considering this second criterion, we concluded that a stop in New Orleans on the deviant Grand Tour was a must. For the city was home to our dear friend, Bennington Ruffel III.

We have known Bennington for many years now. He comes from a very well connected Rhode Island family. In his time, he has been a philologist and a defrocked Catholic priest. He has taught French in a convent school in New York city and been a cocktail barman at the Trump Tower. He was now settled – insofar as Bennington will ever be settled – in the Vieux Carré quarter of New Orleans. Here he spends his time translating the poetry of Algernon Charles Swinburne into Creole and adding to his collection of photographs of child prostitutes by E. J. Bellocq. Such work is not terribly well-paid, of course, but Bennington is fortunate enough to have a trust fund the size of Lake Michigan to fall back on.

Another reason why Bennington Ruffel has chosen to make New Orleans his home is to pursue his interest in voodoo. It was precisely this interest which caused him to 'lose his frock', as Medlar put it, in the first place. The congregation of his small rural parish just outside Allentown, Pennsylvania took a dim view of the discovery that their priest was mixing chicken's blood with the communion wine at Sunday mass. They lodged a number of vociferous complaints with the local bishop. In response Bennington resorted to the rather desperate measure of trying to convince the Church authorities that this event, far from being sacrilegious, was nothing more or less than a miracle of transubstantiation. This attempt failed miserably and he was exposed as a mendacious blasphemer – precisely the qualities which so endeared him to us.

Bennington was good enough to put us up at the Fencing Club, just off Burgundy Street. This is a fine colonial building, white painted with elegant columns and a wide veranda running round both the ground floor and the first. Here Medlar and I would while away the day in wicker chairs drinking mint juleps and enjoying the sweltering humidity created by the proximity of the Mississippi. The river, combined with summer heat, creates an atmosphere which is dank and fetid. Everything here decays and rots in no time at all. Clothing especially can quickly become covered in mildew. I have always found the sensation of clothing, warm and damp with sweat, clinging to my skin and working its way into the crevices of my body, a deeply sensual experience, comparable in its delights to nocturnal emissions or self-soiling.

In many ways the climate is the making of the city. This particular combination of heat and swamp promotes rank and torrid growth. Nature is overwhelming, hostile, and produces the perfect conditions for disease, especially yellow fever, a frequent visitor to the city in the past. Medlar, with his encyclopaedic knowledge of the symptoms of fatal diseases, gleefully gave me the details of what lay in store for the sufferer.

'Ah, yellow fever. Not terribly exciting. Two or three days of backache, rising fever, nausea and vomiting. But then you slip into a deeper febrile state, burning hot, slow pulse, vomiting of dark altered blood. And the skin goes yellow, because of the build up of bile pigment.'

Not only in life, but even in death the position of the city causes problems, as undertakers discovered early on when digging 'the narrow house'. Because the waters of the river rose to within 18 inches of the surface, in order to get a coffin to sink that extra four feet, it became necessary to bore three or four holes in it and have a couple of black men stand on it until it filled with water and reached the bottom of the moist hole. I could not help feeling that having two large black men standing on my coffin was precisely the sort of farewell I wanted.

Some people, rather more discerning than others, were not particularly keen on this idea of a watery grave and had a sort of brick oven built on the surface of the ground. The coffin was introduced at one end and the door hermetically closed. There was an unfortunate side-effect of this however. The heat of the Southern sun on this 'whited sepulchre' tended to slow-bake the body inside, like a soufflé.

When the heat simply became too oppressive, Medlar and I

wandered through the dark wood-panelled rooms of the Fencing Club. A single ceiling fan not only prevented the air in these rooms from becoming stagnant but also drew in the scent of Bougainvillaea and Japonica from outside and distributed it around the room. We were intrigued by the many faded photographs which lined the walls. Here was a portrait of Bastile Croquere, a mulatto, with the reputation – deserved – of being the most handsome man in New Orleans. He habitually wore a suit of the finest green broadcloth and a snow-white shirt with frills like a whore's petticoat. His waistcoat would have made a peacock blush and it was fastened with gold or diamond buttons. Around his neck he wore a wide black stock. He was the haughty possessor of a notable collection of cameos and was widely considered to be something of an authority on them. When dressed in gala attire, he was further embellished by cameo rings, breast pins and bracelets. Bastile was a fencing master and one of the most subtle and dextrous swordsmen of his generation. Unfortunately, he had little chance to prove it as, due to the colour of his skin, he was prohibited from fighting duels in New Orleans.

Not so Gilbert Rosiere, a close rival of Bastile Croquere with the epee, although no match for him in elegance and foppishness. Monsieur Rosiere was a lawyer-turned-fencing master – if he didn't bleed you financially, he could do it literally – and his considerable renown was partly based on his having once fought seven duels in one week. Temperamentally he was so tenderhearted he could not harm a fly. He wept openly and often at the theatre and opera and then killed several men who had the temerity to laugh at this display of emotion. Gilbert Rosiere usually did not need the excuse of a personal slight in order to call someone out. He once fought the Chevalier Tomasi, an eminent French scientist, when the latter was heard to question the status of the Mississippi as the greatest river in the world. Indeed, duelling in nineteenth century New Orleans tended to be characterised by its pointlessness and absurdity, which, it seems to me, are the only wholly justifiable grounds for this colourful ritualistic practice.

Although perfectly content with our life of torpor and excess, we were a little concerned about Bennington. We had seen next to nothing of him since our arrival. He eventually got word to us apologising and saying that he was 'engaged on a project' which he would tell us all about. When he joined us for a light supper of oyster gumbo and snapping turtle fins in a dark rum sauce – as Brillat-Savarin remarked *'The discovery of a new dish adds more to the happiness of mankind than the discovery of a star'* – we related the entire tragic fate of the restaurant and our subsequent exile. Our plight obviously gave him pause for thought, and when he left he told us to meet him the following day at an address on North Basin Street. He had a proposition to make to us.

The next day found us standing outside an impressive 19th century building comprising four stories with bay windows on three sides and crowned by a cupola. From the outside it looked modest enough, painted in an unassuming magnolia. The interior was a little hive of activity. Young workmen stripped to the waist, over-developed muscles glistening with sweat, tools inserted into leather belts, carried lengths of wood or rolls of wire from one room to another. Down the staircase, through this chaos of construction, stepped Bennington.

'I now understand the nature of your proposition,' I told him. 'Did you hand-pick the work force?'

'Of course. But that's not what you're here for.'

'Quelle déception.'

'You two wonderful creatures, as ever, have inspired me. Nobody could ever hope to recreate the Decadent Restaurant. It's inimitable. But I was thinking about opening a bordello, a perfect recreation of a 19th century New Orleans house of ill-repute.'

My unspoken reaction to this idea was one of absolute horror. Bennington went on to explain that he wanted Medlar and me to act as consultants to this project for which we would be paid an absurdly large sum. At this I decided to tell Bennington exactly what I thought of his idea.

'It sounds very exciting. Tell us more, dear boy. What do you have in mind?'

Bennington became very animated.

'Well, I of course would be the madame. Just like Miss Big Knell of Baronne St. You know how good I look in taffeta.'

He moved towards the heavy wood and bevelled glass front door.

'I envisage the entrance here flanked by a couple of figures, probably holding flaming torches in their hands. They'll be known as the Statues of Libertinage.'

Bennington assumed the posture he was describing.

'The general scheme of the decoration will embody a sybarite's dream – luxury and repose – the grotesque and bizarre – splendour without limit, glitter and sparkle suggestive of death and decay. I also want the place peopled with a few figures in flittering attire. From their costumes and manners, they might be visitants from a fabled land. The pictures that hang on the walls, the plated mirrors, the delicately tinted furniture – all will speak of a fantastical nature.'

I must admit I was beginning to feel enchanted, beguiled even, by Bennington's vision. He took us from the entrance hall to a large drawing room which was in the process of being gutted.

'In here will be the bar. It's based on the old Conclave on Chartres St. The back bar will be fitted out as an exact replica of a section of burial ovens or vaults, complete with marble slabs, on which the words 'brandy', 'whisky', 'gin', etc. will be carved. The bartenders will all be dressed as undertakers, and when a customer orders a drink, they'll open a vault in the back bar and pull out a small silver handled coffin filled with bottles of the liquor requested.'

'Hmm. Very novel,' interjected Medlar. 'And what are you proposing to serve?'

'Nothing but the genuine article, Medlar. In fact, come into the kitchen and tell me what you think. I've been experimenting.'

In the kitchen, also an empty shell, there stood a number of dark brown bottles with some glasses standing on a side board. Bennington poured a selection.

'These are all based on the historical research I've done. Genuine New Orleans'

'What a busy boy you've been, Bennington,' I said taking a sip of a suspicious-looking concoction. In general I avoid drinking brown liquids.

'The drinks available in most dives were brandy, Irish whisky and wine. This is the Irish whisky – made by dumping half a pint of creosote into a barrel of neutral spirits. The wine is simply a mixture of three parts water to one part alcohol with colouring and flavouring materials added. If you want something a little more sophisticated, like port, for example, you add prunes, cherries, and burnt sugar, with a little olive oil to provide the old tawny taste. You know what I mean?'

'You may have gone a bit heavy on the creosote,' said Medlar, whose eyes were watering profusely. 'It would make first rate cough syrup, though.'

'I'll make a note of that, Medlar. Now, the technique for making Brandy was slightly different: Into a barrel half full of water you put a pint of flavouring – grape juice or dried fruit – a pound of burnt sugar, a half ounce of sulphuric acid and a plug of chewing tobacco. That provides a sort of bead or sparkle. Then you fill the barrel with neutral spirits.'

'It sounds like the recipe for Coca-Cola,' I observed, as our host swept us out of the bar and into another vast room.

'This'll be the ballroom.'

'For . . .?

'Holding balls.'

'Of course. How foolish of me.'

'I might want to revive the Quadroon balls here.'

'Explain, dear boy.'

'Well, quadroon women are the aristocracy of the Southern mulattos. Lovely countenances, full, dark, liquid eyes, lips of coral, teeth of pearl, sylph-like figures: beautifully rounded limbs, exquisite gait, and an ease of manner. They might furnish models for a Venus or a Hebe. And the Quadroon balls were a refined and well-attended feature of New Orleans society.'

'Really?'

'Don't be silly, Durian. They were little more than slave markets where white men picked up quadroon girls and then ensconced them as mistresses in little houses along Rampart Street.'

'Well worth reviving then.'

We picked our way between dust sheets and found ourselves back in the spacious entrance hall at the foot of the elegant curving staircase.

'And upstairs?' I asked.

'Well, there's nothing to see yet, but I want the rooms up there to be themed, like the *cabinets particuliers* at your restaurant.'

Both Medlar and I immediately bristled at this. Medlar stepped in, almost crackling with indignation.

'My dear boy, our cabinets were not *themed,* as you so crudely put it. They were psychic spaces in which the mind could run free. A perverted playground.'

Bennington ignored Medlar and continued.

'So there'll be the flagellation room, of course. The good folk of New Orleans are long-standing devotees of this practice. There have always been a lot of neurotic and repressed white women in this city for whom it was practically an addiction. A guy called Joe the Whipper used to service their needs. He was a familiar sight on Burgundy St with the tools of his trade in a black bag – switches, whips, and thin flexible metal rods.'

We did not realise it at the time, but we would soon be given an opportunity to ascertain for ourselves the veracity of this statement.

'And the miscegenation room. And the bestiality room,' continued Bennington.

At the mention of the word 'bestiality' I decided to introduce a note of caution.

'Far be it from me to urinate on the camp fire of your enthusiasm, Bennington, but I really ought to advise you against bestiality. The practical problems involved are immense. Do you remember the trouble we had getting that Shetland pony up the stairs of the restaurant, Medlar?'

'Oh, don't! I've never been so shit-besmirched in my life. At least not so unwillingly shit-besmirched. And the mastiffs were very entertaining, but they did drool so. And you have to keep their claws well clipped.'

Bennington was having none of this.

'That's going to be all part of the fun,' he countered. Medlar and I looked at each other and shrugged.

'So what other wonders do you have in mind for your establishment?' I asked .

'Come, Durian. I'll show you. The one room that's finished.'

We climbed the stairs and picked our way between step ladders, pots of paint, lengths of timber and the powerful odour of sweat given off from male torsos.

'I imagine you have no difficulty getting wood in this place,' remarked Medlar.

'They practically give it away,' replied Bennington.

At the far end of a well-lit corridor, we entered a room. The shutters were closed, which meant my eyes took a little while to become accustomed to the dark, but from what I could tell the room had been very simply and tastefully decorated.

'The gallery,' announced Bennington, flicking a switch.

A series of framed photographs around the room were bathed in a gentle, almost yellow light.

'Ah. The Bellocqs!' I breathed, with admiration. I had often heard of Bennington's famous, or infamous collection, but I had never actually seen any of them.

'They are extraordinary.'

E. J. Bellocq was a strange creature. The first thing everybody noticed about him was his lack of stature and his abnormally large head. This encephalic dwarf spent years photographing the inmates of the New Orleans brothels at the end of the nineteenth century. Perhaps it was due to the hideous nature of his appearance, but the whores seem to have developed a genuine affection for and trust in him.

I scrutinised the images, asking Bennington to fill me in on the background to the more striking ones. The first to catch my eye was a handsome but gloomy looking girl.

'Josephine Clare, or J Icebox,' Bennington informed me. 'Worked on Burgundy St. Her madame went by the name of Queen Gertie Livingston and this whore was advertised by Queen Gertie as the coldest in the red-light district, so much so that she offered a prize of ten dollars to any man who could arouse her. Many tried but none succeeded.'

I moved round the room.

'What about this one, dear boy?'

'Oh yes.' Bennington smiled. 'I thought you'd be interested in that one. That's Molly Williams. Came from a brothel at 45 Basin

St. And that is her 10 year-old daughter. Mother and child were sold jointly for fifty dollars a night. A big attraction.'

I picked out another older woman with a young girl.

'No. Not related. That's Emma Johnson. A procuress. She tried selling the fifteen year old girl to a newspaper reporter at a bargain price. When he refused to buy she shouted after him: "You're a fool. The girl's a virgin. You'll never get another chance like this in New Orleans."'

As we continued our tour of the photographs I told Bennington that I knew of someone who was desperate to buy some Bellocqs. Would he be prepared to sell any at some point? He looked at me in horror.

'Durian, are you crazy? I'm quite happy to sell the real thing here. But I'd never sell the art.'

This was precisely the sort of thinking that made Bennington so attractive.

He was opening one of the shutters to release a butterfly which had got trapped in the gallery. I took his arm and looked out of the window along Basin St towards the downtown area with its gleaming tower blocks of glass and steel. My thoughts turned once again to the poetry of Charles Baudelaire, and in particular, the opening lines of *Les Sept Vieillards*:

> Fourmillante cité, cité pleine de rêves,
> Où le spectre en plein jour raccroche le passant!
> Les mystères partout coulent comme des sèves
> Dans les canaux étroits du colosse puissant.

> Teeming city, city full of dreams
> Where in broad day the ghost accosts the passer-by!
> Mysteries flow throughout like sap
> In the narrow channels of the powerful colossus.

How true this seemed of New Orleans! Mesmerised by the voice of Bennington Ruffel, I had seen rise up before me in this house, like the mysterious exhalations from the swamps, some of the hideous figures, the scenes of degradation, acts of violence and cruelty which the city had been witness to.

This reverie was interrupted by his voice once again.

'I know what you're thinking, my dear Durian. The place is just not what it used to be.'

I agreed and he sighed.

'Shall we go and find a bathhouse, to wash the plaster dust from our bodies and the melancholy from our souls?'

\*     \*     \*

As I sat on the hard wooden slatted bench, lost in a welter of steam, it occurred to me that in New Orleans there is little difference between the climatic conditions inside a bath house and those outside. Except, that is, for my proximity to half a dozen glorious naked male bodies. The three of us discussed in detail Bennington's proposed recreation of a bordello. Medlar began by saying just how vulgar, ersatz, artificial and bogus he found the whole enterprise. I agreed but felt that despite those undoubted attractions, there was a danger of the whole thing going the way of the Decadent Restaurant, usurped by the very people you want to upset.

'It's all very Grand Guignolesque, Bennington. In fact it's worse than that. It's a Decadent Disneyland. It may attract the sort of people you want initially, but before long you'll have coach parties of middle managers in plaid jackets arriving from Grand Rapids.'

Bennington looked crestfallen by our comments.

'Does that mean you won't help me?'

'We've been cut to the quick by the keen Blade of Failure, dear boy. We need time for that wound to heal.'

Bennington picked up his towel and hurried out without a word.

'He's upset,' Medlar said.

'You're so sensitive, Medlar. Go after him.'

Which he did, while I engaged the young man sitting next to me in a fascinating discussion. He described himself as a 'circumcision survivor' and was in the process of a prepuce transplant. He was obviously going through a terribly traumatic experience and I took it upon myself, big softie that I am, to console him in the only way I knew how.

It was while I was applying the poultice of consolation to his wounds that I noticed wounds of a different and altogether more interesting kind. Cruel scarlet welts striped his taut and lightly-oiled buttocks, although whatever discomfort they caused young Philippe, he bore the marks of the birch with honour and pride. I remarked on them in a casual manner and he replied that if my taste ran in that direction, he would willingly take Medlar and me along to one of his sister's soirées. These were very exclusive and mainly taken up with that great New Orleans passion – gambling. However he promised us a card game which he guaranteed we had never come across before. I said we'd be delighted to accompany him, although I added the caveat that since the demise of our Edinburgh establishment, we had withdrawn from the canasta game of Life and had become spectators rather than players. We were committed to the role of flâneur, outsider, voyeur. After all, the true Decadent strives to transcend even Decadence itself through boredom, ennui, weltschmerz. He said he understood and that Medlar and I would be welcome as non-playing guests.

Back at the Fencing Club, we sat on the veranda in the warm sticky evening, sipping daiquiris and eating pomegranates, while Bennington indulged his enthusiasm for local history.

'Gambling is of course synonymous with New Orleans. It was precisely for this that the riverboats were invented. One of the most successful was an Englishman, called Dick Hargraves, a slim, dapper man with suave and polished manners. He took to gambling after he won thirty thousand dollars in a poker game with a sugar planter called Dupuy.'

'I can see how that might attract one to it.'

'He spent more than a decade on the Mississippi, with phenomenal success. At one time he was said to be worth two million dollars. Mind you, two million dollars was worth something in those days. At the height of his wealth and notoriety he became amorously involved with the wife of a New Orleans banker and killed the banker when he was challenged to a duel. Then he was pursued by the wife's brother who caught up with Hargraves in a hotel at Natchez. The gambler killed the brother in a desperate fight, then when he returned to New Orleans, his mistress stabbed him and committed suicide.'

'Lucky at cards, . . .' I noted.

Medlar meanwhile was very anxious about what we should wear. Again Bennington provided us with a detailed description of a Mississippi gambler's attire. Typically a gambler would be dressed all in black except for a white shirt. This was cut low at the neck with a loose collar and 'a bosom marvellously frilled and frizzled and only partly concealed by a fancy vest of unspeakable gaudiness fastened with pearl, gold or diamond buttons. At least three diamond rings encircled as many smooth fingers, and another stone, known as the headlight, as large as he could afford, enhanced the glory of the white shirt. In a pocket of the fancy vest was his watch, usually a big gold repeater set with gems, and attached to the watch was one end of a long gold chain which was looped about his neck and draped across his shirt front.' Which is how we appeared as our taxi drew up outside a lugubrious plantation house several miles outside the city. The taxi driver was anxious to spend no more time there than was absolutely necessary. Something about the house and grounds reeked of corruption and decay. The dense verdant vegetation was grotesque. The trees were planted so thickly that sunlight failed to penetrate the canopy of green. The house was in perpetual darkness. The evening air was filled with unearthly sounds.

We were greeted at the door by Philippe and his sister, Lorelei.

'My, Mr Gray, Mr Lucan! You certainly do look the part!' she said inviting us in. She took my arm as we crossed the circular entrance hallway towards the drawing room. She was dressed in a simple, cream-coloured shift of slub silk and was impeccably mannered.

'My brother told me of the great kindness you showed him the other day in the bath house. It was most generous of you, Mr Gray. I think Philippe would benefit greatly from being taken in hand by a more mature man, such as yourself.'

I thanked her for her remarks and added that making her acquaintance more than compensated for any small act of kindness I may have performed for her brother.

In the drawing room, ablaze with candle light, we were introduced to three other guests. A young mulatto woman, an elderly Southern gentleman and a sinister young New Orleans lawyer. His skin was marmoreal white, and he spoke with a slight lisp.

After a number of very sweet cocktails, we moved into the dining room. I looked around the room and had the impression that the subdued lighting concealed much genteel shabbiness. We ate an undistinguished meal – some sort of seafood gumbo – before returning to the drawing room where the four sat down at the card table to a game of faro while Philippe explained to Medlar and me the rules of the game. I failed to follow them then and have no intention of trying to explain them now. However Philippe informed us that his sister was very good at faro and indeed after about half an hour it was clear from the pile of chips at her elbow that she had won handsomely. The players rose from the table.

'And now, time for my forfeit. In our version of faro, Mr Gray, the winner has to pay a forfeit. I hope you enjoy this.'

A low bench, almost like a long narrow foot stool, was brought from the dining room and place in front of the large stone fireplace. Miss Lorelei knelt at one end of the bench and bent forward to lay the upper half of her body along it. The mulatto woman came up behind her, lifted her shift to her waist and pulled her French knickers down to the floor.

As I gazed upon Lorelei's comely white buttocks, the sight immediately brought to mind the description given by André Pieyre de Mandiargues of Edmonde's buttocks in *L'anglais décrit dans le château fermé* .

*Her arse was ravishing . . . nothing about her face shoulders or arms prepared me for the brilliance and whiteness of this arse from which the two domes stuck out majestically like a large ball of sugar under the curves of a narrow waist. It was without wrinkle or fold. Not one spot spoiled the admirable roundness of it. In its smoothness and firmness it resembled the purest marble which brought to mind certain Italian cathedrals . . . These were truly the most sublime buttocks I had ever gazed on! Between them was a very black fur, not unlike astrakhan, which clearly demarcated the beginnings of the buttock line.*

Each player in turn chose one from a selection of slender birch rods which stood by the fire. They delivered three or four sharp stinging blows to Miss Lorelei's rear. Each elicited a whimper from her and soon her buttocks began to redden. What was immediately apparent to me was the expertise of each card player. They obviously had many years experience at this practice and were capable of using the various canes, rods and switches at their disposal to produce anything from a tickle to a cut. The elderly gentleman I noticed was particularly adept and subtle in the variety of his strokes.

Several more swishes from the birch and the redness of the young woman's buttocks had deepened. A number of distinct welts were beginning to appear. Lorelei was now gripping the side of the bench tightly as the tip of the cane come down in an arc and bit into her soft flesh. Her whimpers had given way to a sharp gasp followed by a moan.

After all three players had taken their turn, our sublime hostess gingerly pulled up her knickers. She had earlier admitted to Medlar that flagellation of her backside made her 'lewd' as she put it, for an hour after or so. She liked the birch just to hurt slightly the lips of her sex. Then if she couldn't get a man, she would finger herself 'until the lewdness was dissipated'. She returned to the table slowly, smoothing down her skirt, still smiling and thanking her guests for their kindness.

The game of faro continued and it was clear that Miss Lorelei was in a state of heightened agitation. I watched her hand stray between her thighs from time to time during the game and when the elderly gentleman emerged as the winner of the next round, her impatience to administer the forfeit was almost unseemly. This time however there was a change of routine.

When the old man was duly positioned before the bench, his drooping nates exposed, Miss Lorelei straddled the bench, legs wide apart, and pulled aside the delicate material of her underwear to reveal her lips gaping. She brought her vagina close up to the victim, but was too low for his tongue to reach the goal. I hurriedly gathered up some cushions and pushed them under her divine arse. I saw her wince as this operation was performed. There was no doubt she was still in considerable pain. When her sex was raised to the requisite level, the old man began licking it greedily. At the same time the rod fell on his wrinkled rump which writhed at every blow. Whatever sounds he emitted, whether of pleasure or pain, were muffled by thighs and sex. The lovely face of our hostess clearly expressed that unmistakable ecstasy brought about by an admixture of sensuality and suffering.

The lawyer too seemed in danger of losing control of himself. He was wielding a switch with vicious abandon although it did not seem to cause the old man undue hurt. Perhaps his backside had been inured by many years of such treatment. At one point the mulatto woman laid hold of his flaccid, skinny prick and gave it several gentle tugs. It stiffened a little, and his groans became more audible. These mingled with the frantic moaning of our hostess which was punctuated by the swish and smack of the cane. After several minutes of manipulation from the mulatto, I saw the old man's prick emit a thin trickle of semen onto the parquet floor. Miss Lorelei's writhing lasciviously on the bench was becoming more and more desperate. She took hold of the old man by the head and forced his face into her. But he pulled away. His prick was lifeless, all desire to lick her had gone.

Lorelei, breathing heavily, got to her feet and snapped at the mulatto woman.

'That was very careless of you, Camille.' Then she added, as she stormed out of the room. 'Philippe. Come with me.'

Philippe looked at us and shrugged. He apologised for having to leave us in such a manner but his sister required him. He hurried out of the room and up the stairs after her. It was the last we saw of either of them.


Over the next few days, Bennington's attitude towards us changed markedly. He had obviously been well marinaded in liquor and gently simmering in resentment. By the end of the week he was cooking furiously. It all boiled over one evening at a jazz club in the old town. Bennington lurched across the table at Medlar and me and accused us of treachery. Our failure to support him and his bordello was an act of the grossest betrayal . It was the act of two of yesterday's men consumed with bitterness and envy. Thus far I could not help but agree with him. However, in his frenzy he went on to describe us as 'ungrateful'. The moment he uttered this he realised that he had gone too far. Medlar and I stared at him in horror and disbelief. Then, with the greatest of dignity, I rose from my seat.

'Come, Medlar,' I said. 'Clearly it is our destiny to be cast out, even by those we had invited into our hearts as friends.'

Needless to say, Bennington broke down. Sobs wracked his slightly puffy body as he pleaded with us to stay. But, deaf to his entreaties, I remained implacable. Three and a half weeks later, we left the Fencing Club and headed for Buenos Aires – in search of one of Medlar's most illustrious ancestors.

# BUENOS AIRES

*Esta ciudad que yo creí mi pasado*
*Es mi porvenir, mi presente;*
*Los años que he vivido en Europa son ilusorios,*
*Yo estaba siempre (y estaré) en Buenos Aires.*

This city, which I thought my past,
Is my future, my present;
The years I lived in Europe are illusions,
I always was (and will be) in Buenos Aires.
                                                    (Jorge Luis Borges)

Throughout my late childhood, father and I used to take a Turkish bath together every Thursday evening. We would lie on the warm tiled ledges, sweating like stallions as clouds of scented steam rolled about us, blurring the Alma-Tadema mosaics of the Fornicators of Ancient Rome, while Luther, the family masseur, kneaded father's pale and somewhat fatty flesh to a chorus of contented groans. I would snooze, or read poetry, or listen to father's periodic attempts – rather creditable, they now seem – to introduce me to the mysteries of life as the scion of a thoroughly degenerate family.

Innocent, naked, perfumed days!

Father arrived with a book in his hand one evening. *The History of the Lucans* by T.W. Bamforth. I thought it looked tremendously dull. As if to confirm this, he rested his head on the green volume all the way through his massage. But then, when Luther reached a pause in his pummellings, father turned to me and said, 'Medlar, I've brought this for you. Read it. You will find it most instructive.'

'In what way, father?'

'You'll discover that anything you can think of doing – no matter how extravagant, grotesque or depraved – has been done before by one of your ancestors – usually more elaborately, more obscenely, and more unscrupulously than you could possibly imagine.'

'That is a supremely depressing thought, papa.'

'Do not take it as such. Think of it as a form of permission.'

He placed the volume in my hand.

Luther stood over him holding a curved Japanese sword. My father succumbed for a few moments to the voluptuous sensation of his manservant scraping almond oil off his back with the weapon. Then he turned to me again.

'The Lucans are a mad lot, Medlar. Pleasure-crazed. There's a thing in the blood, a kind of tilt, pointing us very firmly down into the pit.'

'I believe I have felt it, father.'

'Have I ever told you about Uncle Walter?'

'No, father.'

'A man ruled entirely by his prick.'

'I can think of worse things to be ruled by.'

'Quite. But this chap . . . Ah, Luther that's splendid!'

Luther was slapping a floral tonic onto father's pale flanks. Odours of violet and tea-rose, lime, coriander and honeysuckle wafted about us. A final, stinging whack on the buttocks, and father sat up. 'Dress for dinner, Medlar. I'll see you in the Library in fifteen minutes.'


The Library was one of my favourite haunts at Pharsalia. It had Strawberry Hill Gothic bookshelves painted thundercloud blue and enormous leather armchairs with curving Art Nouveau lamps. I spent many a happy afternoon in there, playing indoor tennis with the gardener's boy, while rain pelted the lawns beneath the windows. Father poured champagne and began the story.

'Uncle Walter was born in 1820. He was educated at Eton, which, in case you haven't already found out, is England's Academy of Darkness.'

'I am well aware of it, father.'

'Well, he was too rich even for them. They threw him out. He was sent to the army and had an exceedingly brief career as a junior officer before an aunt very conveniently died and left him a large estate. This allowed him to retire at the age of twenty-one with several millions to his name. He devoted himself for the next sixty years to a life of self-indulgence that Nero himself would have envied. He set off round the world, and became a kind of scientist of pleasure, doing everything to excess, especially if it involved sex. He squandered a fortune in the process. It's said that we lost three quarters of Belgravia through the slit in Uncle Walter's trousers. Which is an achievement of a kind, I suppose . . . But please note: even though he wasted his money, he didn't waste his time. Let me show you something.'

Father put down his champagne glass, and opened a hidden door invisibly carpentered into the panelling. He led me into a small, very luxurious room, finished in sea-blue, scarlet and gold.

'The Secret Library. A place of peace where the world cannot reach you . . . What I am about to show you is its chief treasure. Uncle Walter's legacy. Fifteen volumes of glittering pornographic memoirs. *My Filthy Life*. This, my boy, is an erotic Mabinogion. It was printed in Bruges in the year 1896. An edition of precisely six copies, each most curiously and diversely cased – ivory, tortoise-shell, porphyry, rhino-horn, amber, chameleon-skin. Of these only one has survived – the rhino. It is my proudest possession.'

Father encouraged me to handle these precious volumes – I was astonished by the weight and ruggedness of their binding. They seemed savage, primordial, bestially robust. When I opened one to glance at the narrative, I found Uncle Walter having intercourse in a railway carriage, between Paddington and Swindon, with the wife of a German banker. Father led me back into the main library for an Egyptian cigarette.

'What happened to Uncle Walter?' I asked.

'That has long been a mystery. His last letters were sent from a hotel in Montevideo. But no-one knows where he died. My great-aunt Laetitia, who was Walter's favourite niece, claimed she saw him in a dream. He was crossing the River Plate in a motor-launch, driven at huge speed by Cardinal Newman in goggles and bicycle clips. Walter called out to her – she could hear quite clearly above the roar of the engines – "I'm off to Buenos Aires. La Negrita is waiting!" '

Father let out a stream of Régie Khédive exhaust. 'I've always thought that dream must have a meaning. Laetitia was clairvoy-ant. I remember her trailing about in alchemical costumes, dancing naked around the sundial on midsummer morning. She was a druid high priestess. Won large amounts of money on the horses. You know, I've always meant to go down to Argentina and have a poke around. Never managed it.'

'Who was La Negrita?'

'Another mystery. A waitress? A singer? The wife of a meat tycoon? Or was she the Hindu goddess Kali – the thousand-armed goddess of death?'

Father gave me a significant look. I hadn't the faintest idea what he was talking about.

From that strange conversation, my fascination with Walter began. I gave up indoor tennis, and spent whole days in the Secret Library, studying those magnificent memoirs. Since that time, Walter's example has driven my restlessness, drawn me inexorably along my destined path of excess.


Buenos Aires would have suited him admirably. The city was approaching its peak in the 1890s. Rich, flashy and melancholy, bankrolled by leather and beef, it had buried its sordid past under imported cobblestones and borrowed urban landscapes: avenues, apartment blocks, race-tracks, slaughterhouses, brothels, cemeteries, cafés – all copied from Rome, Paris and Madrid, to make a home for a city of exiles.

Like all the best places it was built on a swamp. The site was discovered by Juan Díaz de Solis, who landed in 1516 and was eaten at once by the Querandí Indians – the start of a long, distinguished gastronomic tradition.

Sebastian Cabot sailed up the same muddy waterway ten years later – baptising it the 'River of Silver', claiming to have found the passage to the 'Kingdom of the White Caesars'. One wonders what he had been smoking. Did these legendary figures – surely the first cocaine lords – ever exist? Cabot returned to Spain without finding out.

In 1536 Pedro de Mendoza came back, equipped to do the job properly – with an army, a commission from Charles V, and advanced syphilis. He built a settlement: the Port of Our Lady of the Fair Winds – Buenos Aires. It did not prosper. Within eighteen months two thirds of the inhabitants were dead from disease, starvation or war with the Indians. 'It wasn't enough to eat rats or mice, reptiles or insects,' wrote Ulrich Schmidl, a Bavarian soldier. 'We had to eat our shoes, leather and everything else.'

On this putrid foundation of failure, Juan de Garay made another attempt in 1580. He was more successful, although Buenos Aires remained a reeking backwater for the next two centuries. Trade with Europe was forbidden, so exports travelled overland to Lima, then by boat to Panama, overland again to the shores of the Caribbean, and finally by ship to Spain. Imports made the same journey in reverse and were wildly expensive. A horse-shoe, in this inverted southern world, cost more than a horse.

Finally, prosperity arrived – through smuggling. Foreign ships sailed up the Río de la Plata for 'repairs'. Their holds were emptied and restocked with new cargoes: leather, mules and slaves. The trade restrictions, now useless, were removed. Wheat, hides, mutton and beef – exported to Europe and America in the first refrigerated ships – turned the city to gold. By the time Walter arrived, our Lady of the Fair Winds was hung with jewellery and ready to receive him.

What took him there? One can only speculate. Perhaps for Walter, as for us, its principal attraction was its invertedness. The way it went into decline from the moment of its founding. The way its citizens reverse night and day. The way their glittering high-octane lifestyle is refined from the heavy black fuel of melancholy.

There is something else to consider. At almost exactly the same moment as Walter's death, in the poor southern *barrio* of Corrales Viejos – an immigrant slum full of lonely bachelors, slaughterhouse workers and stevedores – that magnificent flower of darkness, the tango, was born. Its birthplace was the cheap bars known as *perigundines* or *academias* – where a young man's nights were made sweeter by cheap alcohol, tinkling whores and sixpenny guitars. Surely this was no coincidence. Walter dies, the tango is born. The juggernaut of copulation rolls on . . . I feel quite certain that it was in a *perigundine*, perhaps even in La Negrita's *perigundine*, that Uncle Walter breathed his last. He loved such places dearly.

The tango's musical parentage is a flickering affair. Sired by the milonga out of candomble? Or by the habanera out of a polka? Or possibly a *Gruppensex* of all four? We shall never know. The decisive moment is lost for ever. The tango's godparents are supposedly the *compadritos*, wiry young knife-wielding thugs in high-heeled boots, neckerchiefs and low-brimmed hats. Or any of the vagrants, sailors, herdsmen, factory workers, soldiers, waitresses, cooks, drinkers and tarts who lived in this shimmering estuarine world.

With its aura of danger and glamorous violence, the tango spread quickly. First to the more expensive brothels like Laura's, where the pianist Rosendo Mendizabal wrote a tune for the police chief – an honoured and regular customer. And soon this music for priapic policemen was being played in smart clubs in the Palermo district – El Tambo, El Velodromo – conveniently placed for the city's race-track where the beef millionaires, the 'bovine aristocracy' of Argentina, spent their long, golden-horned afternoons.

Before the tango could be accepted in the highest society, it had to have a spell abroad. In 1911 this rough bastard of the waterfront was brought to Paris by a pair of Argentinian playboys, Ricardo Güiraldes (that exquisitely thin-moustached soul) and the aviator and sportsman Jorge Newbery. They dressed the young apache in a dinner jacket and patent-leather shoes, stuck a gardenia in his lapel and polished his manners to an exquisite sheen. Argentinians made fortunes as dancing masters – 'how we love to dance with this ruined old French nobility', they said – and Paris went mad for the 'jig of whores'. The *Mercure de France* called it 'a sure path to indecency, allowing poses and movements which make the body of the purest woman look infamous.' Is it any wonder that it became so popular? There were tango teas, tango cocktails, and – triumph of decadent transport! – a tango train between Paris and Deauville.

London, New York, Berlin and Rome fell swiftly under its spell. Pope Pius X asked for a demonstration from a smart young couple during an audience. He did not think much of it – 'barbarian contortions of Negroes and Indians' were his exact words. With such backing it could hardly fail.

No doubt this story appeals to us because it is so much like our own. We are like that slum girl in *Flor de fango:*

> *Tu cuna fue un conventillo*
> *Alumbrado a kerosén . . .*

> Your cradle was a tenement,
> Lit by kerosene . . .

Of course the *Mercure de France* was right. The tango is a highly lascivious dance, involving a great deal of symbolic – and not so symbolic – interaction. The Marquise de Pourtalès – a dear friend of Marcel Proust – seeing the tango for the first time, said, 'Surely it's not meant to be danced standing up?'

Yet the erotic power of the tango is only half the story. Guïraldes puts the matter delicately:

*Scent of a brothel. Stink of insolent half-caste girls and men in a fighting sweat.*

*Foreboding of sudden explosions, shouts, threats, ending in a dull moan, a gush of smoking blood, the final protest of useless anger.*

*Red stain, coagulating into black.*

*Fatal tango, arrogant and coarse.*

*Notes flung out lazily from jangling keys.*

*Tango severe and sad.*

*Tango of menace.*

*Dance of love and death.*

There is no finer proof of the tango's liberating effects than the visit of the Prince of Wales, the future King Edward VIII and Duke of Windsor, to Buenos Aires in August 1925. Edward was a limp soul – repressed, stuffy, ignorant – or so the record has it. But was he? . . .

That fateful August, dinner was laid on for him and his travelling companion, the Maharajah of Kapurthala, at a magnificent estancia outside the city. The Argentine cabinet, the chiefs of the armed forces, the British ambassador and naval attaché were all present. After dinner, there was a performance by the greatest of tango singers, Carlos Gardel. Prince Edward was enthralled. A local newspaper reporter captured the excitement of the occasion: 'It is evident that what most interests the Prince in the music is the beat. He reveals an enviable sense of rhythm, since from the start he skilfully accompanied the songs by tapping his feet and nodding his head.' The Prince then ran upstairs to his bedroom, grabbed his Hawaiian ukulele, and joined in with the musicians on a rendering of *Yes, We Have No Bananas*. Can there possibly be a more thrilling tribute to the tango's raw, explosive power?

But we must return to the subject of Walter.

If he did expire in Buenos Aires, we were quite certain that he would have been buried in La Recoleta, the most exclusive cemetery in the southern hemisphere. 'It is cheaper,' say the *porteños*, 'to live extravagantly all your life than to be buried in La Recoleta.' Since Uncle Walter liked everything both ways, preferably simultaneously, it seemed natural to seek him here, in this Palm Springs of the Dead.

It lies off the Avenida del Libertador, a city within a city, bristling with spires, statuary and whirling wrought-iron. We entered its gates excitedly, Durian in his green lizard-skin boots and Cawnpore tiffin suit, I in my tanguero's frac. We roamed the cemetery's avenues in high anticipation, striding between granite bunkers and marble colonnades, pausing in homage by the gateway of the Duarte mausoleum where Eva Perón lies buried beneath two metres of concrete and a thick slab of basalt to prevent the kidnapping of her bones or – one must inevitably presume – the composition of more musicals about her life.

Strange and savage place! La Recoleta is like a thousand Spanish cities crushed into a few acres of stone. But for the impossible prices, one could be tempted to build a home there . . . And yet – our search was long and desolate, we checked every last grave – we were forced to concede that Walter was not among the residents. Or, if he had been, no longer was – pursued, perhaps, like his great-nephew Medlar, by a particularly merciless firm of debt-collectors.

There was only one other conceivable resting place. Almost as expensive, not quite as distinguished, yet ennobled – no, transfigured! – by the mortal remains of the imperishable Gardel. La Chacarita.

The next day, after a breakfast of rose-tea, pelican bacon and passion fruit at the Café Tortoni, we took a taxi to the gates. There we joined the daily band of pilgrims to the tomb of the exquisite Carlos, songbird of the southern hemisphere, dark-voiced crooner of the *arrabales*, who, with *Mi noche triste*, sang the world's first tango song.

> *Percanta que me amuraste*
> *en lo mejor de mi vida*
> *dejandome el alma herida*
> *y splin en el corazon,*
> *sabiendo que te queria,*
> *que vos eras mi alegria*
> *y mi sueño abrasador . . .*
> *Para mi ya no hay consuelo*
> *y por eso me encurdelo*
> *pa olvidarme de tu amor.*

> *La guitarra en el ropero*
> *todavia esta colgada;*
> *nadie en ella canta nada*
> *ni hace sus cuerdas vibrar . . .*
> *Y la lampara del cuarto*
> *tambien tu ausencia ha sentido*
> *porque su luz no ha querido*
> *mi noche triste alumbrar.*

> You woman, who left me
> in my prime of life
> you wounded my soul
> and put gall in my heart,
> knowing I loved you,
> that you were my joy
> my burning dream . . .
> There is no consolation,
> and so I get drunk,
> to forget about your love . . .

The guitar in the closet
is still hanging
no one ever sings
or makes its strings vibrate . . .
And the lamp in my room
has also felt your absence
because its light has not wanted
to light up my sorrowful night.

But to return to La Chacarita. Leaving the pilgrims of Gardel to their devotions, we took a stroll among the tombs. There was Juan Perón, Jorge Newbery, Esteban Hernandez, and many a fine player of polo, chemin de fer, or the bandoneón. Great souls vanished into the darkness! All their elegance and bravado sunk into the wet earth . . .

'Ah Durian,' I exclaimed. 'Look what becomes of us! A few words chiselled on a headstone. A box of rotten bones. Where are their flashing shoes and shining eyes now, their silk shirts and pencil moustaches, their white breasts and rippling thighs?'

Durian gazed at me solemnly. 'You know where they are, Medlar. In the great landfill of history. The shit pit. They no longer concern us. They are rubbish.'

'How I love the brutal clarity of your thinking! 'It's as pitiless as the Sahara, as . . .'

I stopped, amazed. For here, suddenly, in front of us, was a gravestone – unremarkable but for this inscription:

Walter Lucan
Gentilhombre y conocedor
3.XII.1820 – 2.I.1900
'El Casanova inglès'

Tears sprang into my eyes. Dear Walter! Black sheep of the family, fornicator extraordinary, prince of pornographers, shagger supreme! Run to earth at last!

I am not normally one to swell with ancestral pride, but on this occasion I could not help it. Durian remarked, with his unfailing sartorial punctilio, that this spoiled the impeccable line of my cream flannel trousers, but I did not care. Walter was unique.

Fumbling in my bag, I took out a small leatherbound notebook. On its opening page was a poem by Paul Verlaine which I had long ago promised to read over Walter's grave, should I ever be privileged to find it. As Durian poured a simple Voodoo libation, I began to intone:

> My lovers do not belong to the wealthy classes:
> They are workers from suburbs and country;
> Fifteen, twenty years old, unaffected, crude,
> Brutally strong and rough in their manners.
>
> I enjoy them in work clothes, overalls and jacket;
> They don't smell of amber, but only of health
> Pure and simple; their step, slightly heavy, is still nimble,
> Youthful, and solemnly springy.
>
> Their frank, crafty eyes, sparkle with hearty mischief
> And their words of cunning innocence
> Come spiced with carefree oaths
> From those fresh firm-kissing mouths;
>
> Their vigorous pricks and joyous buttocks
> Light up the night, my tool, and my arse;
> In the lamplight and dawn their glorious flesh
> Revive my desire, exhausted but never beaten.
>
> Thighs, souls, hands, my whole jumbled being,
> Memory, feet, heart, back, ears and nose,
> My guts, everything, bawl a refrain
> And hobble a wild jig in their frenzied arms.
>
> A jig, a refrain, lunatic, mad,
> More holy than hellish, more hellish
> Than holy, I'm lost, I'm swimming, I'm flying
> In their sweat, in their breath, as we dance.

I have two named Charles: one a young tiger with she-cat's eyes,
A choirboy turning into a ruffian,
The other, a fine proud cheeky bastard
Shocked only by my dizzying lust for his tool.

And Antoine! With his mythical dick,
My king in triumph, my god supreme;
He rifles my heart with his sky-blue eyes
And my arse with his terrible boar-spear.

Paul, the blond athlete, with a magnificently-muscled
White chest – I suck its hard little knobs like
The Big One down below. François: his dancer's legs
Supple as wheat-stooks; beautiful penis as well!

Auguste, growing more manly by the day
(He was so pretty when we first went to bed)
Jules a bit of a whore with his pallid beauty.
Henri, miraculous conscript, who is alas on his way;

Every one of you! In order or jumbled, alone
Or in a crowd, vision so clear of days gone by,
Passions of now and a swelling future, cherished band
Without number who are never enough!

I closed the little notebook, and we stood in silence while the
klaxons of Buenos Aires rang in the distant air.
   'What a delicate and touching lyric,' observed Durian at last.
   'I knew you'd like it.'
   'Did Walter also indulge in the Greek vice?'
   'He did. Out of thoroughness. But I don't think he ever truly
enjoyed it.'
   'At least he tried. What a noble spirit! . . . Medlar, there is some-
thing I should like to do, if you don't mind. A small homage to
your Uncle Walter . . . Did you notice how the pilgrims to the
tomb of Gardel leave a lighted cigarette in the hand of his statue?'
   'I did.'
   'I feel we should do something similar for Walter.'

'I should love that.'

From his pocket he produced a large Havana cigar. This he lit, puffing cloudlets of blue smoke – then placed it, facing skywards, about the middle of Walter's grave.

A small crowd had gathered, attracted by our pagan rite. They were clearly as moved by its simple beauty as we were. One by one they lit cigars, cigarettes, cigarillos, and planted them in the ground like birthday candles; a hundred little smokestacks for Walter . . .

Sweet tribute to a noble soul! Delicious moment! Enhanced, an instant later, by a voice – a perfume – a presence – from the past.

'There are only two men in the world who can do a thing like that. Medlar – Durian – kiss me, my painted darlings, and buy me a drink!'

'Conchita. My angel. Let me clip you to my soul!'

'Clip me anywhere you like. I'm yours.'


Conchita Gordon – heiress to a gin fortune, uncrowned queen of the Decadent Restaurant, wildly generous and misbehaved, one of our oldest, dearest, most loyal friends. She was not in Buenos Aires by accident. This was all she would tell us. We had to blaze a devastating passage through the Tortoni cocktail menu before she would reveal even a hint of her dark purpose.

'I have a proposal for you. It concerns Walter ... I feel he deserves something special. A feast. A saturnalia. A *grande bouffe*.'

'You have the measure of him,' I said.

'There's a place I have in mind. An estancia. The owner is a friend.'

'A man one can do business with?'

'Very much so. He adores parties. He would pay rather handsomely for a bespoke Lucan and Gray fiesta.'

'That's what we like to hear.'

———=○◯○=———

Several days later we stood in the kitchens of 'La Medusa', surrounded by our staff, and watched a convoy of supply trucks roll up the dusty drive. We counted a hundred and forty of them. We had decided on a somewhat extravagant menu, vaulting the centuries, with a view to commemorating Walter in style. Our host, Antonio de Las Rosas, was anxious on just one count: that this should be the most decadent feast of the senses ever mounted in Argentina. It was a tall order, but a glance at the order of dishes quickly set his mind at rest.

It was a country party, so we set a rustic tone. For the hors d'oeuvre we recreated a bucolic feast given in the gardens of Versailles in 1668. Five enormous tables were set round a fountain. On the first was a mossy mountain representing the earth in its primitive state: it was studded with mushrooms and truffles, cold meat, galantines and pies, and overlooked a lush valley of salads. The second table showed the Kingdom of Neptune, a sugar-glass tank in which sixty varieties of baked fish 'swam' suspended in turquoise aspic. The third was a homage to Ancient Egypt, with pyramids of shellfish and crustaceans. The fourth carried the monuments of the classical world sculpted in goose-liver pâté. The fifth celebrated the Renaissance, with a model of the Vatican exquisitely composed in goat's cheese and smoked peacock. 'It looked,' said an observer, 'more like the enchanted work of fairies than of human beings. In fact no humans were visible when the guests first arrived. Just hands appearing through the fences, holding drinks . . .'

Our main course continued the theme of progress: a one in ten scale replica of the airship *Hindenburg* with 'passengers' assembled from the roasted limbs of a variety of beasts, each forming a different griffin or chimaera: one had an alligator's head on a horse's shoulders, with the torso of a tiger and the hind legs of a boar; another very prettily combined the head of a rhinoceros with the body of a gazelle; there was a sinister snake-headed swan, a sheep in wolf's clothing, an owl-faced poodle with pig's legs, a lovely shark-tailed elephant's head with komodo dragon claws . . . Thirty-six figures in all, stuffed with crushed olives and spiced, minced, hashed, twined, dried, cured, smoked, pickled, beaten and pressed meats. The zeppelin that carried them, an eighty-foot beast of hydrogen-filled silk on a wooden frame, was set, at a carefully timed moment, to burst into flame, very much as the original airship had done in 1937, and deliver its perfectly cooked payload to the party seated at the tables below.

Our theme was completed with a dessert bringing us to the close of the 20th century in the shape of that living symbol of Decadent Technology, the Mir Space Station. Based on Carême's recipe for the Grosse Meringue de Paris – a stalwart at the Decadent Restaurant – with its sweet pastry shell studded with pistachios and macaroons and filled with strawberries and whipped cream, we added a special touch inspired by the pastrycooks of Calabria: a lacing of sugared blood in the cream.

When the main part of dinner was over, and the bloated guests were lolling in flatulent ease under the stars, a hospital trolley was wheeled round, choicely laden with alkaloids, atropines, and opiates. A pair of nurses in starched uniforms (open at the rear) prescribed and gently administered the injections, unguents, potions, pills, powders, pastes, suppositories and spliffs. They prescribed a drug called *chichón* to the guests at our table – each to be taken by a different route. Given first choice, I took the southern polar passage – through the anus. Deft fingers quickly propelled me into a bizarre, twilit world. Whether it was the *chichón* itself, the accumulated angst of months of bankruptcy and exile, the excitement of finding Uncle Walter, or the novelty of hallucinating through my bottom, I find it impossible to say, but I have never had an experience quite like it.

I was riding at dusk across a fertile plain which I knew for some reason to be Thessaly. To my right and left were other riders, cloaked and hooded. We rode hard, with a purpose, the breeze tugging at our clothes. Again, without being told, I knew our destination: Pharsalus. My horse seemed to gallop with enormous strides – sixty or seventy feet at a time – it was practically flying. Once or twice, when I leaned to the right or left, the horizon tilted and we banked like an aircraft.

My fellow riders had long, thick-shafted spears that rested on their horses' necks. At least I thought they were spears, until one turned to me and the end of the thing swung out, its purple onion-domed tip jogging against my thigh.

We dismounted in the mouth of a cave. Firelight flickered from within, accompanied by wafts of foul-smelling air. We left the horses and picked our way in over animal-bones and rubbish to a pallet where a man's twisted body lay, frozen in an orgasm of pain, a hook through its throat. Beyond him, tending a fire and eyeing us with mistrust, crouched the resident of this lair, a hag with pale, spongy, rotting skin, brown teeth, and a straggling beard. Her hair, strands of which hung greasily about her hatchet face, was tied up with a pair of writhing, knotted vipers.

'I know what you want,' she said, her voice rasping like a badly tuned motorcycle engine. 'Your man is there. He'll be ready soon.'

The pot that hung over the fire boiled over. Bitter scents of scorched blood hissed from the embers. Little figures danced up out of the smoke. She carried the pot swiftly to the corpse and, kneeling by the head, slipped the hook out of the throat. She prised the mouth open, then blew three times into the cavity and muttered a spell. Still muttering she picked up a long knife and thrust it deep into the chest in several places, working the blade from side to side to widen the wounds. She lifted the pot and poured in the boiling fluid, a little into each hole, and the cut flesh twisted and brightened as the liquid seared it. Once again I saw tiny wraiths whirling in the smoke that rose over the gaping lips of the wounds.

The witch raised her voice: 'Guardians of the Vast Domain, Keeper of the Infernal Hound, Sisters of Darkness, Ferryman of the Burning Waves! Listen! You know me well! Erichtho is my name. Hear it and tremble! I live among tombs, I visit the dead with life, the living with death, I breathe poison and fire on all who obstruct me. All creatures of sense, in both worlds, fear me. I ask a favour of you. If these lips that call you now are filthy enough with crimes, if I have always eaten the flesh of men before chanting these spells, if I have made it my habit to dis-member bodies still warm from battle, to cut open the breasts of those still living and wash them out with warm brains, hear my prayer! Grant my wish! Send me a spirit. Not a fresh one, but a dried-up old ghost from your deepest caverns . . .'

She lifted her head, her mouth flecked with grey foam, and a misty figure floated up from the earth beside her. It stood looking hesitantly at the body on the pallet and shrank back as if afraid.

'No!' growled the witch. 'You are my servant. You have to obey! Now enter that body at once or I'll cut you loose to wander the earth for ever.'

The ghost drifted down towards the corpse, funnelling itself reluctantly into the mouth. The body shuddered, as if jolted by an electric shock, and the clotted blood in its chest began to boil, heating the blackened wounds, bubbling away into the distant parts of the body, which twitched and struggled as the vital fire entered them. Every limb shook, and suddenly the whole body jerked upright, the eyes wide open, glaring, terrified.

'Speak to me now, wretched soul!' said the witch: 'And when we have finished I shall never trouble you again.'

The dead lips opened, the eyes running with tears. 'You have called me back from the silent kingdom. What can I possibly tell you?'

Erichtho turned her bloodshot eyes towards me. 'The visitor is curious. Speak to him.'

'What does he want to know?' asked the ghost.

'Tell him what acts you committed in life that haunt you even now, in the darkness of death. Educate him!'

'That is impossible. Death is oblivion.'

'Don't try that on me, you stinking little shit! We all know you remember! Now speak.'

The cadaver trembled and swayed, as if it had been struck by an icy wind. Then slowly a few words began to trickle from the black lips.

'My name, when I breathed the sweet air of life, was . . .'

He stopped, gasping, pointed to his mouth and whispered, 'Water.'

The witch swore and hobbled off into the stinking shadows. The ghost stared at me with weary eyes, as if expecting me to speak. I returned his gaze, saying nothing. There was something familiar about him, I couldn't say what. The witch returned with a wooden bowl which she thrust at him impatiently, spilling water over his legs and pale hands. He did not flinch. Instead he looked down into the bowl, drawing my gaze with his, and I saw a wooden building reflected in the water, a long shed on a railway platform. Figures in Victorian travelling clothes were standing about, suitcases at their feet, while workmen in clogs carried buckets and hods to a new brick house in the distance. I felt a violent, twisting pain in my stomach, which pushed me towards the shed. I stumbled in its direction, clutching my belly, hoping not to explode before I could reach the door marked 'Hommes'.

Locked! I tried the next one. Locked again!

Fearful of shitting myself I rushed to the women's. 'Non, non, Monsieur,' screamed out the woman in charge, 'c'est pour les dames.'

'Oh, madame, I'm so ill, – here is a franc, show me somewhere for God's sake.'

'Come here,' she said, and opened a door at the back of the shed. On the door was written 'Réservé au personnel. Défense d'entrer.' In I went, and just in time to save my trousers collapsed onto a wooden seat.

Once the pain had gone, I saw that I was in a long dark room, lit only by dusty sunbeams that came in through holes and joints in the rough woodwork. There were chests, cabinets, lamps, shelves and odds and ends of all sorts, piled carelessly about . The room was still and silent, but through the partition to my right I could hear rustlings, and footsteps, and a French woman's voice saying, 'Vite! Vite!' Doors banged and opened, and just beyond my knee I saw a round hole in the woodwork which let in a strong beam of light. I knelt down and found it was big enough to put my middle finger through – a knot in the wood must have fallen or been forced out. I put my eye to the aperture – and was greeted by an extraordinary sight.

A large brown turd was descending in huge close-up before me, about eight inches from my eye. As it dropped, it disclosed a mass of thickly curled black hair stretched between a fat pair of thighs and great round buttocks. A fart followed, and a tinkling stream of piddle as thick as a cigar. The woman was squatting with her feet on the seat, French style, as if to display her entire apparatus to my inspection. It was more than I wanted to see, but I was riveted. Her anus opened and contracted two or three times, another fart came, then she got up, pulling her petticoats tightly around her. She put one leg onto the seat, wiped herself, let her petticoats fall, and walked out.

I tried to pull back, but found I couldn't. There was a hand on my neck, gripping it strongly and forcing me against the wall. I was about to speak when another woman came in, a peasant-girl about twenty years old, tall, strong and dark. She pulled up her petticoats, turned round, mounted the seat, and squatted. I saw more buttocks, turds and piddle, and felt thoroughly ill.

As soon as she had gone I threw myself violently backwards. Whoever was holding me was taken by surprise, and I brought him down with me as I fell to the floor. For a few moments we wrestled, but my hands slithered on his clothing, which was wet and sticky and repulsive to touch. Then I caught a glimpse of his face and my strength seemed to melt away. It was the corpse from Erichtho's cave.

At the same moment I knew who this old ghost must be that she had called up from the underworld.

Uncle Walter.

I asked him to let go of me. He said he could not. He was bound by inexorable powers to show me, in full, this unforgotten episode of his life.

'You must endure it,' he said. 'You have no choice.'

'How long?'

'As long as I did. Three days.'

'Three days with your eye to that hole!' I was appalled.

He nodded, and the faintest of smiles animated the dead features.

He explained that he had come to the station here at Avignon in 1855, intending to catch a train to Marseille. Seized with diarrhoea, he had gone, as I did, to the staff privy. Then he had seen the knot hole.

'From that moment, I was a prisoner.'

'Did you take no meals, no breaks, no rest?'

'As long as women came to the closets I found it impossible to leave. Sometimes there were long gaps between trains. But the station master's wife made me horny, so we fucked, both here and in the woods. A fine, plump, randy woman. At night I went

167

to a local hotel. I had supper and slept, but only because there were no trains.'

I heard another locomotive approaching.

'Come on,' said Walter. 'That's the express train coming in. Back to your post.'

There was hurry and confusion on the far side of the partition, a jabber of different languages. All the closet-doors banged at once, and I heard English voices.

Pulling her clothes up to her hips a fine young English girl turned her shapely white bottom on to the seat. As she sat down her hand eased her drawers away. A blast of wind, piddle, splash, and it was all over. She was gone. I found myself wishing – somewhat to my dismay – that she had stayed longer. Another came in, pissed rapidly, and went.

Uncle Walter let me sit back. 'Enjoy that?'

'Slightly,' I admitted.

He laughed with unpleasant hollowness. 'You'll love it soon!'

I noticed a trace of Scots in his accent as he said this. Not the most genteel of Scots at that. As he went on this became more marked, and the clipped Victorian syllables grew jagged and saw-toothed. 'You'll be stuck here as I was, glued to the muck, up to your eyes in shite. And then your punishment will start, as mine did. For two years I couldn't see a woman without thinking of her in the cludgie, pissing, shitting and blowin off like a fuckin geyser . . .'

The voice and expressions were becoming coarser every moment, the face was reddening, the wasted limbs filling out with muscle and menace.

' . . . behind that sweet little cuntie is a great raw shittin arse and its comin to get ye, ye're goin right the way up it, cause ye're a lump o' shite yerself, fuckin Medlar fuckin shitehead Lucan and yer nancy boy pal fuckin Durian Gray . . .'

It was no longer Uncle Walter who sat astride me, but John, envoy of Henderson's Debt Collection Agency. John the relentless, John the avenging angel, with hate and destruction in his eyes.

'I've got ye now ye bloody bastard fuckin shitehead and I'm goin to waste you cause you're nothin but a useless bloody heap o' fuckin crap . . .'

His hands had closed on my throat and his horrible red sausage fingers were starting to squeeze. I struggled to remove him, but his strength seemed immense and his fury all-engulfing. All I could do was jerk and wriggle while my lungs clutched at emptiness and my brain spun away in a blood-red vortex of pain . . .

——⊶◉⊶——

R J W Bailey, in his *Psychotropic Plants and Fungi of the Americas*, states that the patient recovers from a *chichón* belter in an 'uneven, slow and bewildering manner'. This observation I can readily confirm. It was a misty morning when I returned to full consciousness. The air smelt moist and agricultural. A hard bumping and rattling jarred my bones. A quick look round – with what felt like deep-fried eyeballs – told me I was in a wooden cart. Durian was stretched out next to me, fast asleep beneath a blanket. Above the sides of the cart I could see the tops of tall hedges, jolting against a cloudy sky.

Where we were going, and to what purpose, bothered me very little. My only concern was to survive the torment of stiffness that ran like rods of iron through every muscle in my body. I supposed that the party was over, the guests all gone home, and we were being transported to Buenos Aires by a peasant on his way to market.

A few miles further on, the cart stopped. I heard the driver step down, his feet crunching gravel. A doorbell jangled. Then a woman's voice rang out. Lighter, more hurried steps crossed the gravel. A head leaned over the side of the cart, blotting out the sky.

'Medlar! Durian! My sweet wicked ones! How perfect to see you here at last! The old place awaits your touch! Come in right away. Your rooms are ready. Have you no bags? Nothing? Ah! My gypsies! I love it! Immense! You must be exhausted. How was your flight?'

Flight? I recalled nothing beyond my encounter with strangling John. Durian groaned and muttered something about 'the great opium empires of the East'. He opened his eyes – winced – and shut them again at once.

Conchita was all concern. 'My dear boys. Come in. You must have some breakfast. Ryan, will you help these gentlemen down from the cart?'

A red face in a tweed cap joined Conchita's in the sky above us. Chapped, rugged hands reached down to haul us out.

We stood like new-born stick insects, wobbly on our legs, blinking in the watery sunlight. Over Conchita's shoulder I could see a large Georgian house built of some dark and forbidding stone. Beyond it was a landscape of hills, fields and lakes that suggested anything but Argentina.

'Conchita,' said Durian slowly, 'would you mind telling us where the hell we are?'

'Mountcullen.'

'And where is that?'

'South West Ireland.'

'Ah. Something told me I was not in the pampa . . . What are we doing here?'

'You're my guests,' she said, her eyes radiant. 'For the next six months, a year, as long as you please . . . Guests and, of course, *consultants*.'

'Conchita, that is an offensive term. Only suburban troglodytes call themselves consultants.'

'Forgive me. Advisors then. Designers. Legislators.'

'That sounds better. On what do you wish us to advise?'

'The grounds of Mountcullen. You're going to turn these dreary acres of pseudo-Capability Brown into something utterly extraordinary – a decadent garden! It will be Ireland's first – possibly the world's.'

'But we know nothing about gardening.'

'I'm not interested in your knowledge,' said Conchita. 'It's your genius I want.'

We found ourselves taken by the hand and propelled, as firmly as our condition would allow, towards the house. Through the open door I looked down the wide hall – filled with flowers by way of welcome – to a view of the lake and hills beyond.

It did not seem a bad place to stay. For a while.

# APPENDIX

# 'THE GOLD STANDARD'

—=∘◉∘=—

*[Editors' note] Appended to Lucan and Gray's manuscript were a number of photocopied pages, headed in violet ink 'THIS IS THE GOLD STANDARD OF DECADENT TRAVEL'. We have traced the text to* My Secret Life, *an erotic autobiography by a Victorian gentleman calling himself 'Walter'. The connection with the adventures narrated in 'Buenos Aires' (in particular Medlar Lucan's nightmarish hallucinations) will be immediately apparent. Whether or not 'Walter' was a member of the Lucan family has been impossible to ascertain.*

I was at A\*\*\*n\*n in the south of France, and went up with my luggage to the station which was being rebuilt. A branch line had been opened the day before, and all was a chaos of brick, mortar and scaffolding. The water closets were temporarily run up in wood, in a very rough manner. A train had just brought in many passengers. I was taken with violent belly-ache, and ran to the closets. They were full. Fearful of shitting myself I rushed to the women's which were adjoining the men's. 'Non, non, Monsieur,' screamed out the woman in charge, 'c' est pour les dames.' I would have gone in spite of her, but they were also full. Foul myself I must. 'Oh, woman, I am so ill, – here is a franc, show me somewhere for God's sake.' 'Come here,' said she, and going round to the back of the wooden structure, she opened the door of a shed. On the door was written 'Control, private, you don't enter here.' In I went rapidly. 'Shut the door quite close,' said she, 'when you come out.' It had been locked. I saw a half-cupboard,

171

and just in time to save my trousers made myself easy on a seat with a hole in it.

It was a long compartment of the wooden shed and running at the back of several privies. No light was provided, excepting by a few round holes pierced here and there in the sides; but light came also at places through joints of the woodwork roughly and temporarily put together. There were chests, furniture, forms, cabinets, lamps, and shelves and odds and ends of all sorts in the shed, seemingly placed there till the new station was finished. The privy seat at which I sat was one end. The privy enclosure had no door, and looking about when my belly-ache had subsided, and I could think of something else, I heard on my right, rustlings, and footsteps, as of females moving, and a female voice say, 'Make haste.' Then doors banged and opened, and just beyond my knee I saw a round hole in the woodwork through which a strong light came into my dark shed. Off I got in a trice and kneeling down looked. It was a hole through which I could have put my middle finger, a knot in the wood had fallen or been forced out, in the boarding which formed the back of one of the women's closets, and just above the privy seat. What a sight met my eyes when I looked through it!

A large brown turd descending and as it dropped disclosing a thickly haired cunt stretched out wide between a fat pair of thighs and great round buttocks, of which I could see the whole. A fart followed, and a stream of piddle as thick as my finger splashed down the privy-hole. It was a woman with her feet on the seat after the French fashion, and squatting down over the hole. Her anus opened and contracted two or three times, another fart came, her petticoats dropped a little down in front, she pulled them up, then up she got, and I saw from her heels to above her knees as she stood on the privy-seat, one foot on each side of the hole. Off the seat then she got, pulling her petticoats tightly around her, and holding them so. Then she put one leg onto the seat, and wiped her bum with two or three pieces of paper which she held in one hand, taking them one by one from it with the other, wiping from the anus towards her cunt, and throwing each piece down the hole as she had done with it. Then looking at her petticoats to see if she had smirched them, she let them fall, gave them a shake, and departed.

She was a fine, dark woman of about thirty, well dressed, with clean linen, and everything nice, though not looking like a lady. The closets it must be added, had sky-lights and large openings just above the doors for ventilation, so they were perfectly light.. The sun was shining, and I saw plainly her cunt from back to front, her sphincter muscle tightening and opening, just as if she had arranged herself for me to see it. I recollect comparing it in my mind to those of horses, as I have seen many a time, and every other person must have seen, tightening just after the animals have evacuated.

The sight of the cunt, her fine limbs, and plump buttocks made my cock stiff, but my bowels worked again. I resumed my seat, and had no sooner done so than I heard a door bang. Down on my knees I went, with eye to peep-hole. Another woman was fastening the closet door. It was a long compartment. When near the door, I could see the women from head nearly to their ankles; when quite near the seat I could not see their heads, nor their knees which were hidden by the line of the seat; but I saw all between those parts.

It was a peasant-girl seemingly about twenty years old, tall, strong and dark like the other. She took some paper out of her pocket, then pulling her petticoats well up, I saw the front of her thighs and had a momentary glimpse of the motte. She turned round, mounted the seat, and squatted. She then drew up her petticoats behind tighter, and I saw buttocks, turds and piddle. She not lift up her petticoats quite so much in front, yet so light was it that the gaping cunt and the stream were quite visible. She wiped her bum as she sat, then off she went, leaving me delighted with her cunt, and annoyed at seeing what was behind it.

Then I found from looking around and listening, that there were several women's closets at the back of all of which the shed ran. It was a long building with one roof, and the closets were taken out of it. Through the chinks of the boards of one closet I could see the women enter, and leave, could hear them piss, and what they said in all of them; but in the one only could I see all their operations. I kept moving from one to the other as I heard their movements, their grunts, and their talk, but always to the peep-hole when there was anything to see, – and there was plenty.

I had now missed my train, the two women I expect must have gone off by it, and for quite an hour the closets were all empty. I began to think there was no chance of seeing more unless I stayed longer than an hour when I knew an express train arrived. I resolved to wait for that, wondering if any one would come into my shed for any purpose, but no one came in. I had eased myself, and covered up the seat; but a strong stink pervaded the place, which I bore resolutely, hoping to see more female nakedness.

There had been a market at A\*\*\*n\*n that morning. Some of the farm-people had come by the train for the first time, the junction railway only having just been opened. I had heard them say so on the platform before I was taken short. Hearing voices just outside my shed, I cautiously opened the door ajar and peeped. Groups of market people had arrived, and were standing outside the station, mostly women with baskets. The eaves of the shed-roof projecting much, gave a little shade from the sun, and they were standing up against it. That told me there would be another train soon; so I shut the door.

In a few minutes close to my door I heard two female voices, 'I want to do caca,' said one of them (in French of course). 'They charge you a penny,' said the other. 'I won't pay a penny, – we shall be home in twelve minutes when the train starts.' 'I shall piss,' said one in broad French. She was close up against the spot where I stood, a board only between us. I heard a splash, then two splashes together. I opened the door ajar again, and peeped. They were both standing upright, but pissing. Both laughed. 'I must do it somewhere,' said one. 'Go over there then, – they won't see you.' 'No I'll go to the woman, and say I haven't any money when I come out.' The next minute she came into the privy with the peep-hole. On my knees I went, and saw the operation complete. Such a nice little girl. She sat some minutes after she had dropped her wax, pulling her petticoats well up from time to time. I had such gloat over her cunt. Once or twice she put her hand under, and felt it.

Spite of my diarrhoea, my prick got so stiff, and I was so randy, that with my eye to the hole and gazing on her round bum and gaping cunt, I frigged myself. My sperm fell on the partition in front of me. I sat looking at it, when I was shitting again. The girl went back to her companion by the shed, and said she had been obliged to pay, and it was a shame. I opened the door, feeling as if I must see the girl's face again. They saw me. 'There's some one in there,' said one, and they moved away.

After that the woman in charge wiped the privy-seat, which I suppose was dirty. Then two or three women came in. Old, and dirty were one or two of them, who sat on it English fashion. I saw their skinny buttocks, and the back-view of their cunts. It sickened me, for they all of them shit, which revolted me. Yet the fascination of the cunt made me look at all of them, – I could not help it. One woman had her courses on, and moved aside a rag to do her needs, – that nearly made me vomit. That woman squatted on the seat.

For a quarter of an hour or so no one came. A trumpet, a railway-bell, and a hubbub, then told me the express train was coming in. Then was hurry, and confusion, a jabber of tongues in many languages. All the closet-doors banged at once, and I heard the voices of my country-women.

Pulling her clothes up to her hips a fine young English woman turned her bum on to the seat. It came out of a pair of drawers, which hid nearly her buttocks. As she sat down her hand eased her drawers away from her cunt. Splash, trump, and all was over. The hair of her cunt was lightish. She was gone. Another came who spoke to her in English, and without a moment's delay pissed, and off she went.

Then a lady entered. As she closed the door I saw a man trying to enter. She pushed him out saying in suppressed voice, 'Oh! for God's sake are you mad? – he can see from the carriage-window.'

'Not there sir,' I heard the woman in charge cry out. The door was shut, and bolted.

The lady, young and handsome, stood quite still, facing the seat, as if overcome with anxiety; then feeling in her pocket, took out some letters, and selecting some, tore them in half, and threw them down the privy. That done she daintily wiped round the seat with a piece of paper, lifted up handsome laced petticoats, and turning her rump towards the seat daintily sat down. She had no drawers on. She must have fancied something, for she rose again directly, and holding her clothes half-way up her thighs looked carefully at the seat. Then she mounted it, but as if she scarcely knew how to do it, stumbled and bungled. She stood upright on it for an instant, and then I could only see half-way up her legs. At length the bum slowly descended, her petticoats up, and adjusted so as to avoid all chance of contamination. I saw the piss descending, but she was sitting too forward, and the piss fell splashing over the edge of the seat. She wriggled back opening her legs wider, and a pretty cunt with dark hair up to her bum-hole showed. My cock stood again. She jumped off the seat, looked down the privy, gave her clothes a tuck between her thighs, and went off.

Then came others, mostly English, pissing in haste, and leaving, and bum after bum I saw. Then came a woman with a little girl. She was not English, she mounted the seat, and cacked. Whilst doing so she told the child to 'pi-pi bébé' on the floor, which she did not. When she had finished she wiped her arse-hole with her finger, – how she cleaned the finger I didn't see. She then took up her child, held her up over the seat with her clothes up to her waist, her cunt towards me, and made her piss. The tiny stream splashed on the seat, and against the hole through which I was looking – a drop hit me on the eye. How funny the hairless little split looked to me. To think that her little split might one day be surrounded with black hair like her mother's, and have seven inches of stiff prick up it. Her mother's hair was black, and she had a moustache.

Again a row. 'Not there Monsieur, – l'autre côté.' 'It's full God damn it – I am not going to shit myself,' said a man in English. 'Vous ne pouvez pas entrer,' – but he would. A big Englishman – a common man – pushed the woman in charge aside, and bolted the door muttering. 'Damned fool, – does she think I'm going to shit myself!' He tore down his trowsers, and I moved away, but heard him let fly before he had sat on the seat (he had the squitters), and muttering to himself, he buttoned up and left. I heard him wrangling with the woman in charge.

Instantly two young ladies entered, sisters seemingly, and English, – nice fresh-looking girls, both quite fair. One pulled up her clothes. 'Oh! I can't sit down, – what a beastly place, – what beasts those French are,' said she, 'dirty beasts, – call the woman, Emily.' Emily looked outside. 'I can't see her, – make haste, or the train will be leaving.' 'I can't sit down.' 'Get on the seat as those dirty French do, and I'll hold your petticoats up. Take care now, – take care.'

'I shall get my feet in it,' said she. 'No you won't.' She stood fronting me, and pulling up her petticoats till they looked as if tied round her waist in a bundle, showing every part from her motte, to her knees, (my eye just at the level of her bum), and saying, 'Don't look and laugh' – but laughing herself, she got on the seat. A prettily-made creature, not stout, nor thin, with a cunt covered with light-brown hair. She squatted. I saw the bum-hole moving. 'I can't do it like this,' she cried, 'with all this nastiness about me, – are my clothes falling down?' 'No, – make haste, – you won't have another opportunity for two hours.' Out and in went the anus again, the pretty fair-haired quim was gaping, the piddle began to fall. She wanted to piddle badly enough. I said aloud in my excitement at seeing her beauty, 'Cunt, cunt.'

The girl got upright, I could now only see half her legs. 'Hish! Did you hear?' said she. Both were silent. 'It must be the woman in the next place.' 'It sounded like a man.' Then she spoke in a whisper. 'No it can't be.' She squatted again laughing. 'It's no one.' Her evacuations dropped and off she got. 'You go, Mary,' said the other. 'I only want to pee, and I'll do it on the floor.' 'The dirty creatures, why don't they keep the place clean?' Squatting I watched her face. It was all I could see then, and suppose she pissed. I only saw her hitch up her clothes, but nothing more.

Then the closet-woman came, and wiped the seat grumbling, women opened the door whilst she was doing so, then others came in, and for half an hour or so, I saw a succession of buttocks, fat and thin, clean and dirty, and cunts of all colours. I have told of all worth noting. The train went off, and all was quiet. I had again diarrhoea, and what with evacuating, the belly-ache, and frigging excitement, felt so fatigued that I was going away. As I opened the door the woman was just putting the key in. She started back as she saw me.

'Are you ill?' she said. 'Yes.' 'What a time you have staid, – why did you not go?' Then all at once, as if suspecting something, she began looking at the backs of the women's closets, and found the hole, and looking half smiling, half angry, 'You made that,' said she. 'No.' 'Yes you did.' I declared I had not. 'Ah! Méchant, méchant,' said she (looking through the hole), and something about the chef de la gare. 'You have been peeping through.' 'Certainly.' I was so excited, so full of the adventure, that I had been bursting to tell some one, and talk the incident over. So in discreet words I told her about the man, and the woman, and her letters, and other incidents, till she was amused, and laughed. Then spite of my illness my lust got strong as I looked at her, for she had a cunt. She was a coarse sun-tanned, but fine stout sort of tall peasant woman about thirty-five years old. So I told her of the pretty little splits, and nice bums I had seen, all in select language. And I so longed, Madame. 'Oh! if I had had them in here.' 'Ah! no doubt.' 'Or if you had been here, for I wished for you.' 'For me? – ah! ah!' – and she slapped both her thighs and laughed. 'Mais je suis mariée, moi, -ah! méchant, méchant.' 'Here is another five francs, but I must have a kiss.' She gave it seemingly much flattered. I said I should come the next day. 'Ah! non!' she must tell the Chef, it was her duty, – it would be useless if I came for that hole.

We talked on. She was the wife of a workman who it seems travelled up and down the line almost continually with officers of the railway, and only came home about once a week, or ten days. She had no children. Whilst talking my diarrhoea came on. My paper was gone, she produced some from her pocket, and simply turned her back whilst I eased myself (the enclosure had no door), as if it was the most natural thing in the world. Finally after saying that she would not dare to let me in the next day, yet on a promise of ten francs she said she would, and volunteered the information, that by an early train many farmers' wives would probably arrive for the market, that many would come by the line just opened She must report the hole to the Chef, – it might cost her her place if she did not, and it would be stopped. I kissed her again, and whispered in her ear, 'I wish I had seen you sitting, and that you had come in here afterwards.' 'Ah! mon Dieu que vous êtes méchant,' she replied laughing, and looking lewedly in my eyes – and I went off. I had been there hours.

I took my luggage back to the hotel, eat, got refreshed, went early to bed, awakened quite light and well, and got early to the station. She was awaiting me and directly I approached, took no notice of me, but opened the door, looked in, closed it and walked away. I guessed what the game was, loitered about till no one was on that side, then slipped into the shed, the door of which she had left ajar. Soon after in she came, and gave me the key. 'No one is likely to come,' said she. 'It's only the Chef and Sous-Chef whom the seat was made for, and now they have new closets on the other side of the railway; but if they should, say that you saw the door open and wanting the cabinet used it.' Then off she went, but not till I had kissed her, and asked her to go and sit on the women's seat. I found the peep-hole plugged up, and could not push the plug out. I hesitated, fearing to make a noise; but hearing a woman there, my desire to see cunt overcame all scruples. With my penknife I pointed a piece of wood, applied it to the plug, and taking off my boot to lessen the noise, hit it hard with the heel, and at length out tumbled the plug. I expect it fell down the seat-hole.

Two well-to-do French peasants came in. One got on to the seat and to my annoyance shit and farted loudly, both talking whilst stercoratious business was going on, as if they had been eating their dinner together. She had huge flappers to her cunt, – an ugly sight. The next pissed only, and I was rewarded by a sight of a full-fledged one, and a handsome backside. One had a basket of something for the market which they discussed. One said they must give the caretaker a halfpenny, and they evidently thought that a great grievance. What had they been in the habit of doing in such necessities previously I wonder. One said she would take care not to pay it again. The closet accommodation at railways in France was at that time of a very rough primitive kind, seats had not long been introduced.

For half an hour all the women were of that class, many quite middle-aged. More women came into that privy, than into the others I could hear. (I had given the keeper the ten francs.) They were mostly full-grown, and had thickly dark-haired cunts. Almost all the women mounted the seats, some pissed over the seat as they squatted. I was tired of seeing full-grown cunts, disliked seeing the coarser droppings, and left the peep-hole weary, but the cunts took me back there.

Two sweet-looking peasant girls came in together, they must have been about fourteen or fifteen years old, only, and both had slight dark hair on their cunts. When they had eased themselves they stood and talked. One pulled her petticoats up to her navel, the other stooped and looked at her cunt, and seemed to open it, then the other did similarly. They spoke in such low tone, and in patois, that I did not understand a word they said. Both girls wore silk handkerchiefs on their heads, had dark blue stockings and white chemises. They were beautifully formed little wenches, and I longed for them with intense randiness, but restrained myself from frigging, determining to find a woman somewhere to fuck, and I felt again an overwhelming desire to tell some woman of the sights I was witnessing.

I missed a good deal of the talk when women were together, owing at times to noise in the station; yet the women who came by express trains talked very loudly, nearly always. They seemed in a scuffle of excitement, ran in, eased themselves, and ran out quickly; and if two together, spoke as if they had not the slightest suspicion of being overheard.

No one had yet noticed the peep-hole, though so large. The women seemed mostly in a hurry, pulled up their petticoats, and turned their rumps to the seat directly they had shut the door. At length a splendid, big, middle-aged woman came in, and was most careful in bolting the door, then turning round towards the seat, she lifted her clothes right up, and began feeling round her waist. I wondered what she was at. She was unloosing her drawers. She was dressed in silk, had silk stockings on, and lace-edged drawers [drawers were only then just beginning to be worn by ladies]. Peeping from between the drawers every now and then was the flesh, but nothing more suggesting what was behind.

Apparently unable to undo them, she broke the fastening with both hands, and the drawers fell down to her knees. What a pair of lovely thighs she had, but I only saw even those for a second, for her petticoats fell. She disengaged her limbs from the drawers, pulling the legs one by one over her boots, rolled up the drawers tightly, and put them into her pocket. Then pulling up her petticoats as she stood sideways I had a glimpse for a second of a splendid bum, and the edge of the hairy darkness. Then she dropped them, stood still and looked. I felt sure she was looking at the hole, and drew back. When I looked again the hole was plugged with paper. I did not move it till I heard she had gone.

Although now growing tired of seeing backsides, and cunts gaping in the attitude in which cunts look the least attractive; yet I felt annoyed at missing the sight of this lady's privates, and could scarcely restrain myself from pushing the paper through. I thought she told the closet-woman, for I saw that woman look in directly she had left.

For a full hour I then saw nothing. I had not heard a train, and looked at my watch. It had stopped. I peeped out of the shed-door, saw no one, went out, put my head round the corner, and saw the care-taker knitting in the shade. She saw and followed me at my beckoning. The train had not arrived, it was one hour behind time.

She came into the shed. 'Talk low,' said she, 'for some one may be there and hear.' I told her of the lady and her drawers. She said the lady had told her of the hole. We both laughed, she called me, 'Sale, – méchant,' but did not stop my kissing her. I got more free, and from hinting got to plain descriptions. She took no offence. I told her of the two girls looking at each other's cunts, that I longed to be kissing one of them; that the sight of their pretty slits made me long to have one of them (I used chaste words). 'Or both,' said she. 'I'd sooner have you, for I like plenty of hair.' In the half-light I saw her eyes looking full into mine. She laughed heartily, but stifled the noise, and I was sure that she felt lewed. I kissed her, and pinched her. 'What fine breasts you have.' Then her bum. 'Laissez-moi donc.' Then my hands went lower. 'My God let me feel your cunt.' 'Hish! talk low,' said she. The next minute I was feeling her cunt. 'What hair, – delicious, – ah!

foutre, – faisons l'amour.' But she coquetted. 'Now don't, – if any one should come, – I won't,' – whilst gently I edged her up against the side of the shed, one hand full on her cunt all the while. 'You must not, – mais non.' Then out came my prick, and she felt it. Another minute's dalliance. 'Let me put the key in the door,' said she, 'and then no one can let himself in.' She did, and in another minute standing up against the shed, we were fucking energetically. Didn't she enjoy it!

We had just finished when we heard the train-signals, and off she went. 'Come back.' 'Yes, yes presently.' Down to the peep-hole I dropped, holding my prick in my hand; there already was a cunt pissing in front of me. English I guessed, for she was half sitting on the seat. Then for half an hour was a succession of backsides and quims, mainly English and Americans (a first-class train only). I knew them by face and dress, and nice linen, and because they nearly all sat or half-sat on the seat, whilst others mounted it. I wished my country-women had mounted also, to enable me to see their privates better. They nearly all piddled only. There was a restoration at the station. Nearly every woman of other nationalities shitted, they wanted I guessed, full value for their ten centimes.

Another woman plugged the hole with paper, a knowing one who did it the moment she entered the privy. I pushed it away directly she had left, she grunted much, and was a long time there.

Then I saw the cunts of an English mother and four daughters, just as the train was ready to go. They had from what they said been eating and only just came in time. The girls looked from fourteen to twenty years of age, the mother not forty.

Luckily some one before must have fouled the seat. The mother entered first with the youngest. 'Stop dear,' said she in a nice quiet voice, 'the seat is filthy.' She opened the door, put her head out, and I expect called the woman. Returning, 'Get on to the seat, dear.' 'How Mamma?' 'I'll show you,' and she got up, but daintily hid her limbs from her child. 'Look the other way dear.' The girl turned her back, and then she pulled up her clothes, and I saw the maternal quim and piddle. Then she helped the girl up. 'I'll tell Clara what to do,' said the mother, 'take care of your clothes dear,' and she left the privy. The girl did take care, and showed her nice little bum and unfledged cunt charmingly. Piss only again thank God.

The other girls entered afterwards. Each smiled as she mounted. Would they have smiled, had they known my eye was so near their bum-holes? Piddle only. Then the fourth followed and piddled. The train moved off, directly they had left.

The care-taker soon came round to the shed. I told her all, talked baudy, soon at her I went, we fucked, and after our privates had separated we talked. There would not be another train for some hours, she usually went home to dinner, any one could go to the closets then without paying. I wanted to go home with her, but she refused it. She would be there at *** o'clock, an hour before the *** p.m. train. Yes on her honour. I gave her a louis. "How good you are," said she. She was surprised. I had promised her nothing for fucking her. We both wanted that, and therefore did it, – that is all.

I went to my hotel, eat and drank, and before the time, let myself into the shed with a key she had given me. She came back early, and dropped her eyes. She was a stout woman with large waist and haunches, a sturdy, plump, well-fed peasant with good eyes, and bronzed cheeks, a good bit of flesh for a fuck. I wonder how I had cheek to attack her for all that. Now however I had felt her hard buttocks, and in my randiness her cunt had seemed divine. I had whilst waiting, pulled down a dusty, long, cushioned seat from the miscellaneous heap of things, and we sat down on it. I began feeling her. 'Let me see your cunt.' 'Haven't you seen enough women's?' 'No I must see yours.' 'Tell me about the two girls again, – I think I know them," she said. On being asked I told her, and a lot more. 'Que vous êtes méchant, you men, – do you so like looking at women when they are doing caca?' 'No I did not, – I could not bear it, but their thighs, their lovely round bums, their cunts, anything to see those parts, – I will see yours,' I got her to stand up; and then with the modesty like that of a newly-married woman permitting her husband, she let me see. It was not a bit in the manner of a harlot. I looked at her wet quim in the dim light, and soon we fucked again.

Then we questioned each other. What she had to say was soon

told. Her husband had for many years held his post, he was here, there, and everywhere, and came home once a week if lucky, but generally once in ten days, and then had an entire day to himself. She had the post of privy-opener given her, because of her husband, and made more money than he did though only in pennies. It would be a good deal more now, if they let her have it all, for there would be more trains, but they would divide it, for there were to be closets on both sides. 'Then you only get fucked (not mincing words now), once in ten days.' 'That's about it,' said she laughing. 'You long for him to come home?' 'That's true.' Just then we heard some one in the privy. I looked, she would not, and went off with a moistened quim to attend to the people. A train was coming in.

Back came she afterwards, and we talked for two hours. My cock was ready. I laid her on the form, and straddling across the seat, and holding her legs up across my arms, entered her quim. But she nearly fell off the seat, it was so narrow; so again up against the wood-work, we copulated. She was well grown, so it was not difficult. She took to the fucking, as if I had a right to it, and she liked it, but I always disliked uprighters.

Again we sat down and talked. 'You won't want your husband now.' 'He comes home to-morrow,' and she showed me a little scrap of dirty writing-paper with, 'On Tuesday' written on it, and a mark at the bottom with a date. 'That's his mark,' said she, 'he can't write. I've been frightened to-day, for sometimes he comes without writing, – I'm here to meet him.' We then kissed each other. 'You are very handsome,' she said. 'You are beautiful,' said I. 'Am I really?' 'Yes, and fuck divinely.' 'Do I really?' said she in a most flattered manner.

'Directly he comes he fucks you here?' 'He's never been in here in his life, but he makes love directly he gets into our rooms,' she replied in a quiet tone, as if she'd been telling a doctor her ailments. Still we sat and talked. The shed had been only built for storing things quite temporarily, the privy was for the Chef, but it had not been used by any one for some time. The hole in the wood could not have been there long. How made, she knew not. She must have noticed it, had it been there long, for she washed the seats continually. Holes were often made by men in the sides next the women's closets, they bored holes to look at the women, she wondered 'pourquoi mon Dieu,' why they wanted to see when they were doing their nastiness?

Again through the peep-hole I saw such a nasty, dirty, frowsy, beshitten backside, and the chemise of an oldish-rabbit-arsed female, that a disgust which had been gradually intensifying, made me indifferent to seeing any more, and females came and went without my even looking. I now sat on the cushioned though dirty form comfortably (before I could only sit on the privy-seat), waiting for the privy-woman to come back. But curiosity still got the better of me. An express train came in with English and Americans, and I looked. People who come by train are always in a hurry, sometimes they have wanted to ease themselves an hour or more, and then let fly before almost they get their breeches down, or their petticoats up, very often indeed they let fly at random over the seat. Then those following them finding the seat dirty, mount it to avoid fouling their clothes.

'It's beastly,' I heard in a high pitched American tone. Two nice, young, shortish girls, were there. 'Let's go to the next one.' 'There is some one there, – there is not time, – get on the seat.' Up got the girl with her face towards me. 'Not so Fanny, – turn round stupid.' 'I can't, – this will do,' said Fanny, and pissed out of a dear little cunt covered with lightish brown hair, set in delicious buttocks. I put my eye close to the hole, and the piddle spashed into it, for she peed on to the back of the seat, and how she wanted it! 'Make haste Fanny.' 'Oh! I did want so, – I've not done it all day. Then up got the other in other fashion, close to my peep-hole, and watered! In shape of bum, thigh, and cunt the two were as like as two pins, pretty, fleshy little bums, round little thighs, plump as a partridge. I was so lewed I could scarcely resist a desire to call out to them, and say I had seen their charms. The last one turned round when she had done, and got down. 'Oh!' said she, 'there is a hole in the wall.' 'Oh! if –' said the other. That was all I heard, for they quitted the privy like lightning, putting their heads together, and lowering their voices to a mumble, and talking earnestly. Afterwards when the train had left, back came the keeper to me, and said the young ladies had told her of the hole.

She begged me not to go there the next day, for her husband might arrive by any train; but I did, and had her. I dined at the hotel, and at night having nothing better to do, strolled towards the station smoking a cigar. – The attraction of cunt I suppose did it. She had said that she left directly after a particular train, and some other woman took her place for night-work. There she was, – no her husband could not arrive now till next morning. Let me go home with her, on no account would she. Between the station and the town were some woods being made into public gardens. Walking there against her will and in the dark, I talked lewedness to my heart's content, and at length had her with her back up against a tree. 'Lay down, – it's quite dry,' said I, and on some coarse sort of dryish herbage, – I could not see what – I fucked for the last time and on the top of her. We got up whispering adieu, when we saw dimly a man and woman who began the game. She was scared 'Let me go, and you stay,' said she. Just then their vigorous love-making made a great noise. Off she went, I in a second or two followed and overtook her. 'C'est une sale putain,' said she, 'she has commenced coming here of a night to meet men going to the station – it is disgraceful, – I shall inform the Chef to-morrow.' Then the closet-keeper kissed me, and went off with her cunt wet, and a Napoleon which I insisted on her accepting.

The next morning I left A***, but could not keep my promise, and went to her at the station. The blood rushed into her face, she looked scared, and shook her head seemingly in a funk, and I departed by the next train.

I have often wondered at the affair, and at that woman. Had she been a whore? Did she in her husband's absence usually have a bit of illicit cock? My impression is that she was steady and honest; that I caught her just when she was hot-blooded, that my doings were so baudy, that her lust was roused, and so she was helpless at my first attempt, and then having slipped, thought she might as well have all the pleasure she could. She had no children. French women don't see so much harm in an outside fuck or so. I had promised her no money, had offered no inducement whatever but my prick. It was lust which stirred lust, and we gratified each other. What more natural?

The adventure left me in an unpleasant state of mind, for I could not bear at that time anything connected with the bumhole. With women, if I thought of that orifice, it destroyed voluptuous associations. Now I could not look at the prettiest woman without thinking of her shitting and farting. The anus came into my mind when dancing, dining, or talking and whether randy or not; and when the tingling in my prick made me look, and long for a woman, thinking what a leg she had, what thighs and quim perhaps, my mind went to her bum-hole spite of myself. I was punished heavily for my peeping. It was a year or two before my mind recovered its balance, and I was able to think of their sexual organ and its beauty and convenience without reference to its unpleasant neighbour!

One of the first I saw bogging, was a pretty shortish English girl perhaps seventeen years old, but with a backside that many a woman might have envied. She also had a lovely skin and complexion. She neither got on the seat, nor quite sat on it, but rested in a half-standing position, and turned out a light-brown turd a foot long. I saw also her hand feeling once a plump little cunt. She could not find the paper to wipe herself with, felt in a pocket, took out her handkerchief, felt again, found nothing, put her hand in her bosom, took out a letter, and after opening it, tore off a piece about three inches square, replaced the letter in her breast, and wiped her bum with the torn fragment.

When I got back to my hotel that day, the first female I saw was the young lady. I could not keep my eyes off her. She was a sweet-looking creature; but all that I could think of, was that great turd, I thought of it till mad with myself, I left the table, and got out of her way.

Fortunately the greatest number only piddled, – I shall always like to see a female at that function. The attraction to the peephole was of course to see the hidden charms, the fat round buttocks, the lovely columns of flesh which support them, the split, the love-seat, the seat of pleasure, the cage for the cock, the cunt, that mysterious aperture leading to the organs in which a future human being is formed and secreted, and to which man gives life by fucking, – fucking, that divine orgasm, that creator which ought to be praised daily in our prayers and hymns, and which a false refinement (born of lewedness) calls indecent and beastly, if it be alluded to.

At this time I had already written much of my early life. This episode of the temple of Cloacina dwelt so much in my mind, that although I disliked it, yet at the first hotel which I stopped at for a few days afterwards, I wrote this out, and a great deal more. I recollected the face, form and performances of every woman I had seen; but the repetition of similitudes was wearisome, and I obliterated quite one half, if not more. I had doubts if I should not omit the whole, but a secret life should have no omissions. There is nothing to be ashamed of, it was a passing phase, and after all man cannot see too much of human nature.

# ACKNOWLEDGEMENTS

The editors would like to thank Mike Abrahams for the portrait of Medlar Lucan and Durian Gray on page 15, and John Hoole and Mervyn Heard for their help with other pictures.

They would also like to thank the following for permission to quote from Copyright material: Stephen Mulrine (translator) and Faber & Faber Ltd, for the extract from Moscow Stations by Venedikt Yerofeev, quoted in 'St Petersburg'.

Neil Rollinson, for his poem 'Sutras in Free Fall', from his collection *A Spillage of Mercury* (Jonathan Cape, 1996), and the North American Space Agency for the 'CUVMS' procedure, quoted in 'Cairo'.

Editions Gallimard for the passage from *L'Anglais Décrit Dans le Château Fermé* by André Pieyre de Mandiargues, quoted in 'New Orleans'.

Dedalus made every effort to contact the other rights holders, without success, and would like to hear from them.

# THE DECADENT COOKBOOK
## MEDLAR LUCAN & DURIAN GRAY

—⸺∘◕∘⸺—

Book of the year choice for Nigella Lawson in *The Times* & John
Bayley in *The Standard.*

'The chapter headings say it all: Corruption and Decay; Blood,
the Vital Ingredient; The Gastronomic Mausoleum; and I Can
Recommend the Poodle. This is a not a normal cookbook but a
slightly sinister and highly literate feast of decadent writing
on food. There are dishes from the tables of Caligula and the
Marquis de Sade, a visit to Paris under siege (when rat was
a luxury), some unexpected uses for cat food and some
amblongous recipes from Edward Lear.

There should be something here to delight and offend everyone: the recipes for cooking with endangered species looking
particularly tasty.

Mouthwatering.'

Phil Baker in *The Sunday Times*

'Lucan and Gray, whose fruity monikers may strike some as
being suspiciously apt, have concocted a fabulous and shocking
assemblage.'

Christopher Hirst in *The Independent*

'Arresting, too, is *The Decadent Cookbook* (including a recipe for cat
in tomato sauce).'

Nigella Lawson in *The Times Books of the Year*

'The putative authors are Medlar Lucan and Durian Gray, a bit of
a tip-off: the medlar is a small, brown fruit, eaten when decayed;
the durian fruit tastes good but smells like sewage. These two
coves left editors Alex Martin and Jerome Fletcher to tidy up this
compendium of hideous repasts, taboo-busting banquets, and
surprisingly sensible fare, accompanied by passages from
decadent literature: menus courtesy of the Marquis de Sade,

J. K. Huysmans, King George IV, the Grand Inquisitor and other gluttons.'

*The Independent on Sunday*

'Not just fun but useful, containing workable recipes for Panda Paw Casserole, Cat in Tomato Sauce, and Dog a la Beti ("prior to being killed, the dog should be tied to a post for a day and hit with smallsticks, to shift the fat in the adipose tissue"), myriad blood sausages recipes, a recipe for aye-aye, of which some 20 remain in the wild, and stories by Louis de Bernieres, Huysmans, inevitably, and Charles Lamb on sucking pig.

Not as you will have gathered, for the squeamish.'

Nicholas Lezard in *The Guardian*

'Fancy boiled ostrich? Cat in tomato sauce? Or virgin's breasts? The droll compilers trawl ancient Rome and other OTT times for kitchen oddities, mixed with literary off-cuts and pungent commentary. Delia Smith it ain't.'

*New Stateman & Society*

'Start with a glass of blood, to set you up: recipe given in Jean Lorrain's short story, helpfully included.'

John Bayley in *The Standard's Books of the Year*

'If meat is the hard-core-of-food-as-sex, *The Decadent Cookbook* is a walk on the wild side, a book for those who scorn not only the Prohibitions of Leviticus but also the dictates of common sense, good health and kindness to animals.'

John Ryle's City of Words Column in *The Guardian*

'A scholarly work, cleverly disguised as a very amusing read, from Medlar Lucan and Durian Gray. 223 pages of about every kind of weird or simply repugnant food from the Romans to the 19th century, with intriguing recipes for boiled ostrich, roast testicles, boneless frog soup and other obscure delicacies. There's even a whole section on cooking with blood. The perfect gift for posh friends: it is the kind of book they always have in their loo.'

Richard Cawley in *Attitude Magazine*

'Forget Prue Leith and Delia Smith the cookery manual that every Venue reader needs is *The Decadent Cookbook*. If your palate is a little jaded, if you thought you'd tried everything, then this is the book to make your smart dinner parties go with a bang (and several yech! s). The pseudonymous authors have trawled through the world's great works of history and literature to assemble a truly sumptuous feast of decadent dishes and ghastly gastronomy.'

Eugene Byrne in *Venue*

'An extravagant, shameless and highly entertaining book that could change the course of contemporary cuisine.'

*The International Cookbook Review*

'As a cookbook, this is as authentic as the authors' Christian names (two varieties of rather decadent fruit) and is actually a very funny anthology of the best and worst excesses in gastronomy. Excerpts from literature are peppered throughout, from the gastronomic desires of the Marquis de Sade to the curious case of a man obsessed by cat food. A passage from *L'Anglais Decrit Dans Le Chateau Ferme* starts: "The shit was very tasty. I helped myself to as much of it as I had the fish sperm." Whole chapters are devoted to sausages, and blood, with a number of excellent recipes featuring that most decadent of fluids. For those of a morbid and liberal persuasion, this book is essential reading. For those who also possess streaks of cruelty, it would make a lovely gift for a vegetarian or a maiden aunt.

*Wicked recipes, but not for the faint-hearted* Dead decadent.'

Bill Knott in *Eat Soup Magazine*

'WARNING! Do not read on if you fall into the category of vegetarian or squeamish faintheart. Ever wondered what panda paw casserole smells like?

What about the wafting odours of cat in tomato sauce, or New Zealand parrot owl pie? "Mmm lovely," is unlikely to be the response unless you are nasally-challenged. Entire chapters of this tome are devoted to blood and other bodily fluids, with one titled: "I Can Recommend The Poodle". Check out the recipe for Manila Hot Dog. Take refuge in the risque literary excerpts that pepper this most outrageous of cookery books.'

Ann Donald in *The Glasgow Herald*

'*The Decadent Cookbook* represents the Stephen Milligan/Ozzy Osbourne school of cookery. Written by the pseudonymous Medlar Lucan & Durian Gray, this should provide a trusty handbook for those who can make oenophily sound like a per-version – provided they have enough like-minded companions to invite round for a traditional Roman orgy or a Marquis de Sade dinner.

Recipes are provided for both occasions, along with instruc-tions for perfect black-blood soup (with goose-giblet garnish) and "I can recommend the poodle" as one of the chapter headings. Much time, research and, I suspect, a copious amount of whisky has gone into this brilliant, black and funny book.'

Lizzie Fairrie in *The Erotic Review*

'*The Decadent Cookbook* is guaranteed to make your table a talking point again. But be warned, with chapters entitled "I'll Have The Poodle" and "Marquis de Sade's Sweet Tooth", this is no ordinary fare. The authors' advice is to forget traditional food snobbery – there's no good reason why dogs, cats and even rats shouldn't appear on your supper table, apart from a lack of good recipes. To remedy this deficiency, they offer instructions for dishes such as flambed liver of dog and cat in tomato sauce. But the height of culinary delight is reserved for endangered species. How about panda paw casserole, black bear sausages, or parrot owl pie (based on a recipe for parakeets by Mrs Beeton)? So there you go, all the perfect ingredients for an evening of sparkling wit and champagne. Just remember to tell your guests to bring a doggy bag.'

David Batty in *The Big Issue*

£9.99/$13.99 ISBN 1 873982 22 4 224p B. Format

# THE DECADENT GARDENER
## MEDLAR LUCAN & DURIAN GRAY

—=•◉•=—

'extraordinary'

> Ian McEwan

'Following the success of *The Decadent Cookbook*, this is another generous dose of decadent writing, arranged in sections such as the erotic garden, the cruel garden, the fatal garden, the garden of oblivion. Contents include a guide to poisonous plants, Octave Mirbeau's *Torture Garden*, Edgar Alan Poe on being buried alive (a remote gardening hazard), and Lord Rochester's *Farce of Sodom* or *The Quintessence of Debauchery* (printed in 1689, incinerated 1690; the characters' names still wouldn't be printed in a newspaper). Not a book to give as a present to the unsuspecting, but ideal if you want something pervy for the potting shed.'

> Phil Baker in *The Sunday Times*

'You may remember the authors' previous work, *The Decadent Cookbook*, highly recommended in these pages. This time, they have done even better: they must have done, for under normal circumstances my interest in gardening is not even detectable at quantum level, yet here they enthrall.

Plans for sinister, corrupting gardens, planted with poisonous plants such as Hellebore, Hemlock and Meadow Saffron. Contains the full text of Rochester's play Sodom – for production in the garden theatre, of course – itself an uncanny prolepsis of contemporary fears about Aids. The only gardening book you will ever need.'

> Nicholas Lezard in *The Guardian*

'. . . for the jaded gardener who has seen it, done it and mulched it all, is *The Decadent Gardener*. Lucan & Gray have been called in by Mrs Gordon to redesign the Mountcullen acres. The book describes and explains their ambitious plans for the estate. A cruel, synthetic and fatal garden are only the first of their transformations. As with their previous book, *The Decadent Cookbook*, the authors reveal that there is a dark side to an activity widely thought to be the preserve only of ladies in sensible shoes.'

Anna Pavord in *The Independent's Christmas Books*

'Lucan and Gray trawl the murky depths of cruel and mad kings, kinky writers and eccentric little-known deviants of all kind. In vanished gardens, real or imagined, they trace every decadent inflection.'

Book of the Month in *Attitude Magazine*

'subversion and perversion at first seem inimical to a fresh-air culture of allotments, hanging baskets and compost heaps. Yet, as this bizarre and often shocking book makes clear, vices of all sort lurk among the mixed herbaceous borders and nature is not always a pretty sight. Lewd, cruel and sometimes very witty, it is more a manual for those gardeners who would rather offend than impress their neighbours.'

James Ferguson in *The Oxford Times*

'Travel into the dark side of the most suburban and safe activity. Ignoring the ponces in green wellies and old women with rubber kneelers and trays of marigolds, Lucan & Gray concentrate instead on such green fingered fuck-ups as the Emperor Nero, Cardinal Richlieu, the Earl of Rochester and the even more bizarre sex and death, decay and daisies world of the Chinese emperors. Free cutting: "Small fragments of human flesh, caught by whips and leather lashes, had flown here and there onto the tops of petals and leaves." '

*Loaded Magazine*

'Following their *Decadent Cookbook*, Lucan & Gray return with an equally entertaining account of their horticultural activities. Drawing on historical inspiration such as Nero's ideas for cheap and practical illumination (human torches), they propose a range of fantastic gardens in which poisonous and narcotic plants, Priapic statuary, erotic landscaping and rude vegetables abound.'

*Scotland on Sunday*

£9.99/$13.99 ISBN 1 873982 82 8 252p B. Format